Aunt mary!
Yoou're my fav Aunt!
Don't tell Jane!

THE LiGHTNiNG LEGACY

EMiLY CYR

Published by
Crushing Hearts and Black Butterfly Publishing, LLC.
Novi, Michigan 48374

This book is for the one I lost and will never get to hold.

Special thanks to Sarra and Jolene.

Your friendship has meant the world to me.

Bravery is the capacity to perform properly even when scared half to death.

—Omar N. Bradley

PROLOGUE

Mil

IT WAS COLD in death. I knew it would be. It wasn't the real thing though. This was a dream. And this was his way. His way to tell me what I should do with Delaney. It wasn't the first time he had come to me in a dream, but I had an odd sense of finality, as though this would be the last time. His way to tell me his will. I follow the old ways of the Druid, not this warped witchery of a godless Coven.

Feeling brave, I slid my eyes open to find I was in snow, a large expanse. I stood in the middle with snow falling all around me. I looked down and saw I was in

1

my nightgown. Yet I was not near as cold as I should be for this weather. Aye, this was his doing. Taranis, god of the storm.

"Oy, Taranis, I'm here. What do ya want with an old witch?" It wasn't like me to taunt a god. Oh wait, yes it was.

Laughter filled the large expanse, seeming to run over my skin, lighting every nerve ablaze. Still, I did not see him. Then I felt his hands cup my face. They were warm and the gesture was loving. Yet I knew this god. I knew he had his own agenda and nothing would stand in his way, not even my beloved Delaney. Slowly, he revealed himself to me. He was a tall man, at least in this form. I was not some new babe, naive enough to think this god had only one form. Though this was the form Delaney would describe to me when he visited her in her dreams. She was so young then.

"Millea, is that any way to talk to the god of old?" His tone was scolding, but it held a note of amusement.

I would not be cowed, not even by a god.

"Taranis, you meddle with my child. I have raised her since she was just a wee thing. That girl carries my heart. I do not take kindly to this prophecy, nor do I take kindly to you trying to harm her. I just want her to live a full life, without complication."

I was breathing hard; clearly this conversation was a long time coming. Behind the god, lightning struck the snow-covered Earth. The flare of light echoed the flash in his eyes. I'd angered him. I was not afraid though.

"Millea, you knew this would happen. And you know what comes next. She will die. Fear not, old woman, she will rise. And when she does, she and her mate will unite the two separate lines into one. And, she alone will end the reign of these weak beings called witches."

His tone had calmed, yet still held his eastern European accent.

I felt the warm trails of my tears as they rolled down my cheeks. I turned my face from him. I couldn't have this conversation. This talk of my adopted daughter willingly sacrificing herself. I felt his too-warm finger slip under my chin, coaxing my face to look up at him.

"Oh Mil, she is of me too. Do you think I would let any harm come to her?"

His voice was low and controlled and I saw something in his dark gaze, something that looked much like love. My emotions that had bristled softened somewhat.

"Will she hurt?" It was a mere whisper. I couldn't help it though.

"Yes. Pain beyond anything she could imagine. Sometimes to grow and evolve we must have so much pain it breaks us. Then, we will be forced to find a way to put ourselves back together. That is what will unite her power and that will make her a true Druid of old."

His words were firm, but I could not accept them.

"Take her pain. I'll beg you if I need to. I'll do anything! Please take her pain away."

My voice was shaking and I had no care.

He raised his eyebrow to me as though he was contemplating my words.

"At her moment of death, I will take her pain as a gift to you. But, she must hurt. She must break. I cannot help her until the moment she shatters."

My lips pursed and, just as I was about to speak, he held up his hand in a motion to silence me. Just then, I noticed the snow was swirling around us as though we were the eye of a storm.

"I have need of you. I have one more task for you."

He ran a finger down my cheek in a way that a lover did.

"This will be your last."

With his words, a knot formed in my stomach.

"What is that?" I asked in a weary tone. I realized I was tired, so tired deep within my bones.

"I need you to not fight the wolf who comes to you this day. I need you to give up your life for Delaney."

The breath I hadn't realized I was holding left my body with a whoosh. I had to leave my daughter to be killed. For Delaney, I would do anything. I nodded to him. It was all I could manage. I had questioned him early on in our interactions as to why I should heed his instructions. His answer was simple. If I didn't, my fate would be worse than death. I could feel the pressing weight of his power. The only thing I could compare it to was, well, God.

"Here, take this, and when you feel pain or fear this will ease it. Also, this coin will give your power what it needs in order to do what it was meant to do. This coin will gift your powers," he said, handing me a small golden disk.

I raised it to look at it more fully. The only thing depicted on it was what looked to be a wagon wheel. *What my power was meant to do?* What did that mean? I looked up to question the god but, much like his nature, he was gone, not even leaving behind footprints in the snow. I sat down in the fluffy white mass and fingered the ridges on the coin and waited to wake up. Waited to meet my fate.

THE LETTER WAS easy. I poured everything into it. She needed to be prepared for what was to come. The interfering god never said she couldn't be warned. I also made a plan for my power. I knew what the God meant by gifting my power. And I knew who to give it to. The thought would have made me giggle had the situation not been so grim. I stowed the letter in a security deposit box and would leave a note telling Delaney where to go to find it. I shoved the coin and the small key in my pocket and grabbed a piece of paper, readying to write Delaney a message. What should it say? Sorry, I'm dead?

My phone began wailing over the quiet of my house, completely adding to the tension I was already feeling. I groaned, but answered anyway.

"What do ya want?" I spat at the receiver.

"Hey, Mil. Are you up for having guests? I thought I would bring a few friends by..."

"Ah, Laney girl. Fine and when you get here we can talk about you moving."

Maybe I could just avoid this whole thing if only she would agree to it.

"Yes, Mil, I'll think about moving. We should be there in about five hours."

Her tone was clipped.

I knew she would never run, not anymore. She was growing in her strength. I winced at the thought because I wouldn't get to see her with that power. I choked back the emotion I was feeling. I did not need her questioning me.

There was a firm knock at the door. I could feel power and menace thrumming and I knew who it was.

"Laney girl, I have to go. There is a man here to clean my carpet." It was a lie, but it was the best I could come up with as my mind and nerves were just about shot.

"Oh, okay. Bye." Her tone was disappointed and it alone almost caused me to break.

"Bye, my love," I choked out and hung up the phone. Another knock sounded at the door. Apparently death was on a time line.

"Ah, hold on to your panties. Don't you know I'm old? Give me a damn second."

I took a deep breath, settled my resolve and opened the door.

Standing before me was a tall man with stunning green eyes and nearly black hair. He eyed me warily.

"Well what do you want, wolf?"

His eyes went from bright green to glowing.

"Old woman, what did you tell her about the prophecy?" he said, barging in through the door and nearly knocking me over.

"Everything," I lied. I had a shot of fear that this male could be her mate. However, I remembered Taranis said he would not let harm come to her.

"Well then," he said, facing me.

I walked into the kitchen and raised my hands to him. He froze at the sight of my glowing hands. I was an Earth Witch and as much as I would die this day I wouldn't do so quietly. I pulled not from my core like most witches, but directly from the Earth itself. His eyes went incandescent with fury. I had no time and I knew it. Then he did something I did not expect. He rushed me. There were no words with this male. I let go of the Earth magic I'd gathered. He hit me with the force of a train. The force at which my head connected with the ground was nearly enough to cause me to black out. I was slightly dazed and felt his hand circling around my throat. My hands flew to his, trying to no avail to pry him off of me. But, alas, I was old and he was far too strong. I could use my magic, but the God's words rang over and over in my head. His grip tightened and he leaned down to snarl in my ear.

"She will be mine to do what I want with. She will carry my babe."

With what little energy I had left, I shoved a hand into my pocket and grabbed the coin that, at my touch, soaked into my skin. Instantly the pain was gone. I felt a surge of exquisite power. It was time to send my power off. And I knew who to gift it to. With my last bit of strength I dug deep inside myself, grabbed a tentative hold of my power, and sent it out of myself.

I met this man's eyes and with my last gasp said, "She will never be your mate. It can never be."

His eyes went wide and his grip tightened yet more. He continued to yell at me, but my hearing was gone. The blackness swirled around my vision, reminding me of the swirls of snow from my dream. I didn't want my last thought to be of this wolf. So I thought of Delaney playing with a small plastic tea set. I thought of her smile and I smiled. This was for her. Everything was always for her. I let go and slipped into the darkness. Ah, there was the snow.

DELANEY HAGEN

ONE

POMPEII. I REMEMBERED reading about Pompeii when I was in high school. I couldn't recall which of the four high schools I was attending when I read about it though. That's neither here nor there. I remembered seeing people frozen, encased in stone. It never had much of an impact on me until now. It made me wonder if their souls were trapped in their stone prisons. Could they feel the world around them? Were they in an unyielding cell? I liked to imagine I knew them. *Hell, maybe we are family.* I knew them, because I was one of them. My prison's walls were made of drywall, reinforced by self-loathing and hatred.

I felt myself falling down a hole I might never be able to escape from. It's a rabbit hole, Alice. That's what I tried to convince myself of, that at the other end of this abyss of blackness and pain, there was a world of wonder. But all I could see were the walls of my confinement and wolves at every turn. I was becoming cynical, someone I barely recognized. I rolled over onto my back and stared up at the ceiling, trying to rid myself of any thoughts of a land of wonder, because my life held little magic. I tried like hell to grasp the edge of this hole. I knew I couldn't hold on. It was a futile effort on my part. I realized belatedly that I had let go of the edge a long time ago, and now I was falling with little hope that someone would catch me. Frankly, I wished I would slam into the Earth and break into a thousand shards of myself. I closed my eyes and tried to picture it.

It had been four months since that night. The night I died. I had this internal storm I couldn't seem to quell. It writhed just below the surface and I had no idea how to stop it. I spent my days locked in this room and my nights being forced by Mitch to change into my wolf form and hunt. I hated what my life had become and I felt broken. I rolled over again, this time I buried my face in the mountain of pillows, trying to suffocate myself. Well okay, not really. But now, with this new life? Punishment? I saw little good. So death by pillows didn't sound too bad to me.

I feel like I have another being inside of me, clawing at the sides of its cages trying to pry its way out. I had to see the face of the man who did this to me almost daily. And the man I love was locked away under the threat of death. My life had become something unrecognizable and something not worth living.

I heard footsteps coming closer to the room I was kept in. I froze, trying to calm my heart rate. The locks rattled and clicked. The door was in desperate need of some WD-40. It howled as though it were in pain. I could smell the man on the other side and it made my hackles bristle. It was him. The ass fuck who did this to me. I did my best to be nice. Okay, that was a lie, I didn't. The prick killed me. I wasn't likely to forget about that, nor any of the other things he had forced on me since. I tried and failed to stifle a shudder at the recent memories.

He was in the room now. I could hear his breathing hitch and smell his growing arousal. It disgusted me. He walked over to the side of the bed and sat down. I wouldn't show fear, nor would I shake at the sight of him.

He smoothed a hand over my hair down to my back. *Don't throw up. Or wait, maybe I should.*

"Delaney, come on. I know you're awake."

God, even the sound of his voice was cocky. Even though, this was his "sweet" voice. Clearly he wanted something. I knew what he wanted though. I turned my head to look at him and the look in my eyes must have been more than words, because it caused him to withdraw his hand from me. I hated when he was gentle with me. It wasn't like him. He was just doing it to get on my good side. The thought of that nearly made me bust out in whoops of laughter. I think he was cemented on my bad side. His hand went to the back of my head. He grabbed a fist full of hair there and yanked me from my laying position until I was kneeling on the bed, supported only by him. The pain would have been excruciating while I was a human, now it was merely an annoyance. Nonetheless, I gritted my teeth to keep from yelling out.

He leaned into my ear and growled, "Is this how you want to start today? You want to get on my shit list? Because I'll tell you, Delaney, I could be so good to you." He trailed his other hand down my face, past my throat to my breast.

My skin crawled with disgust. I focused on the power in my core. Since my change, the well that had always been the focus of my power had grown. I pulled from it. This time the power rushed to me easily. I focused on his touch and pushed my power to my skin. He withdrew his hand as though he was burned. I smiled at him sweetly. He then wrenched his hand back and slapped me across the face. My cheek burned with the pain of his strike and my mouth filled with blood from clamping down on my tongue. His hand at the back of my head gripped tighter and he pulled me back even farther. I was bent so far back I began to feel pain in my thighs.

"Dammit. That hurt," I spat at him.

"I'll close my hand next time," he hissed.

"Mitch, god dammit, what are you trying to accomplish?" I gritted out through clenched teeth. My hands instinctively went to his on the back of my head, trying to steady myself and pry him off of me.

"You could make this easy. You could just give yourself to me. But, no. You fight what could feel so good. And now I'm going to have to take you to my room for punishment."

His room. *Please no*. His words were like ice water. His room was something out of a horror movie.

"Mitch, what do you want?" I really did not want to spend another night being punished. My body began shaking at the memory of the one night I was in his room.

Without warning, he grabbed me between the legs. My breath left me. Ice pulsed through me. My shorts were only made of light cotton and I had no panties because Mitch refused to give them to me. I could smell how much he wanted me and the scent of it made my skin crawl. My hands flew from my hair to his hand grasping me and I dug my nails in. The scent of blood filled the room as I scored my nails that were curling into tiny claws along his wrists. I felt his warm blood form a trail from his wound down my thighs. He didn't even flinch at the pain. That pissed me off. I began pulling power from my core.

He began to squeeze me hard as he said, "This, Delaney. You give yourself to me without shocking me or causing me pain. Because I'm getting to the point where I'll take it from you. Remember what is at stake here. You know he lives, but I can change that."

Just as fast as he grabbed me, he pushed me to the bed and let me go.

I felt him get off the bed and walk to the door. He absentmindedly rubbed his wrists in pain. At the gesture, I felt my lips quirk up into a smile. God, even that felt like a victory. He looked down at his hands and stopped. It was too late though. It was sad that something so trivial felt like such an accomplishment.

"Until your attitude improves, you won't be allowed to hunt," he said. Then I heard him lock the door. That felt like a reward. I curled up on my side, but wouldn't cry. A tear trailed down my cheek despite what I wanted. My life was rubble and I simply wanted to lay down in the wreckage and waste away with the tatters of my life.

THREE DAYS, MITCH didn't come back for three blessed days. The new moon was nearing and I could feel its draining pull on me. I, unlike the other werewolves, could shift from my human form in the span of a breath. However, it was still painful. I'd found a love of running though. Darting around trees and dodging any obstacle in my path was like a high for me. Mitch never let me out of his sight, but when he did allow me to hunt, it was exhilarating. But the act of the kill always discomforted me. I could never revel in it like the rest of Mitch's pack. Speaking of those assholes, they lived for the kill. For me, being in my wolf form, it wasn't about the kill, it was more about letting the wild part of me go to the forefront and really letting loose. It was about more than death for me; it was so much about life. But the thought of warm blood coating my tongue sent a shiver through my body. I hated that part of me.

There was a knock at the door.

"If you're not Publisher's Clearing House, you can go fuck yourself." Okay, I know I wasn't being very nice. I'd run out of fucks to give.

I heard Mark's low grumble of distaste. *Ah yes, I guess he got the short straw today.* I heard the sixty-seven locks click open and the chains fall away. I might have tried to leave this cell a few times, hence the Shawshank-style confinement.

"If you could be nice just once, Delaney, that would be great."

Mark's dull, monotone voice oozed over my skin. The guy really gave me the willies. He had his back to me as he pushed into the room, pulling a cart with what I knew would be my lunch.

"Oh, well, Mark, then I wouldn't have near as much fun!" I quipped back at him. "Did your master let you off your leash? Were you a good boy? Did you kneel at his feet and suck his…"

"Shut the fuck up, bitch!" he snarled, whirling to face me. His plump, craggy face was red. Though he was short and slightly round, he was not altogether displeasing.

Mark was Mitch's third in the pack. He nearly tripped over Mitch's heels, he clung so tight to his master. That was basically all I knew about him. I smiled at the expression on his face. He was so mad. His little beady eyes were pinched and his mouth was just a small white line that slashed across his face. He was slightly limping. Clearly, he had been hurt yesterday at the pack meeting. Oh, the meeting I couldn't go to. But there was something more with him. He wasn't his cocky self. I needed to find out what had happened to knock this man down a peg.

I eyed him as he placed the plates on the edge of the bed. His eyes met mine and held there. Looking at him in the eyes he would see as a challenge, but damn it, he dropped his eyes in submission. I had to clamp down on the urge to go for his neck. I don't think he even realized the significance of what just happened. My eyes widened, then narrowed.

"Just what happened at the meeting, Mark?" He stiffened at the mention of it.

"I was challenged for third."

Oh shit. I didn't think he would really answer me, he never answered me. None of the wolves did. They were told that they should avoid talking to me and if they ever touched me Mitch would rip them apart. Or at least that's what I assumed because of their treatment of me. Then again, I'd only come into contact with about ten of them.

"Oh Mark, what happened? Where you hurt?" I tried my best to keep calm and not push him away. I wanted information and if I had to play nice to get it, I would.

"Dillon," he spat the name as though it were a curse. Then his face twisted into an expression that made me think the name left a bad taste on his tongue. "He challenged me and won. And Mitch did nothing but stand there and watch."

This was how a pack worked. Mark was really close to Mitch yet he had allowed the challenge to take place. *Dissension in the ranks?*

My mouth hung open with shock. Dillon was further down in the pack. He was a tall man, but not ripped. He was toned, more of a runner's body than that of someone who sculpted his body though. Moreover, he was what I believe to be the definition of a sociopath. He had meal duty once. After he shoved me against a wall, Mitch never let him near me. Mitch and Dillon were very similar, but Dillon hurts creatures just to see them in pain. Had Mitch not been close by, I'm not sure what would have happened.

I shivered at the memory.

I glanced up to see Mark studying me. He clearly had his ass beaten and, damn it, I was not feeling sorry for the creepy bastard. I just wasn't. Ugh.

I smiled softly at him and said, "He's an asshole, Mark."

Damn it, I was feeling sorry for the greasy, beady-eyed creature.

He eyed me warily. I sighed.

"Look I don't like any of you. Your dick of an alpha killed me and has the man I love locked up somewhere. And not one of you will help me. But, beyond that, Dillon…" I trailed off as I heard something just outside of the room. It passed, but I lowered my tone marginally. "Mark, Dillon is sick in the head. Like he skeeves me out. I'm sorry you lost, but I think you're lucky to still be breathing."

God, why was I being nice to him?

"You're not always a cunt, are you?" he replied, walking to the door.

"Why Mark, I think that's the nicest thing you have ever said to me," I said to the closing door.

Mitch's pack was huge. There were more than thirty members. None of whom were female. I was the only one. Not that I would be here for long, I hoped. I'd only met about ten of the pack members. Mitch would only let the top members of the pack near me because he couldn't trust the rest of them. I think the reality was that I would be able to overpower them. There was a small part of me that thought the rest of the pack really didn't know what he was doing to me. I often wondered if they would object to it.

I opened the covered dishes and found a tuna fish wrap and chips. Hey, it was food, right? My mind slid back to what Mark told me about Dillon. I didn't know why this conversation seemed like it could be a way out, but it was possible I could use Mark. I mean if I were actually nice to him, maybe he would leave the door unlocked or give me tidbits of information.

I began to formulate a plan. Ugh, that wouldn't work. If I did get away, Mitch would just come after me. There would be nothing to stop him and he has proven killing people was not above him. I'd only tried to kill Mitch once. The same night I tried to escape.

I couldn't kill him. There seemed to be this invisible force stopping me. That's when he informed me that a wolf couldn't kill its maker. Along with my night-long punishment, my hopes of getting out on my own were utterly dashed.

I ate my lunch, trying desperately to think of a way to get away. This wasn't the first time I tried to come up with a plan. However, I felt like this was the last chance I would get. Over the months, I tried to connect with the mysterious man in my dreams, but since my turning, he had been missing in action. I guessed I would be on my own with this one. I got up and began to pace the short length of my confined little room. Maybe walking would get my brain going.

Thirty minutes later, nothing. All I could think about was Mark and how pissed he had looked. Okay, so if I did somehow get him to turn on Mitch and help me get out, where would I go? Well, I would have to find Reid. Then what? *Ugh! This is impossible!*

I moved the plates off the mattress and placed them by the door. I went to sit on the bed. Cupping my hands, I did the only thing I could: I pulled my lightning from my core. In my cupped hands, there sat a tennis ball-sized ball of lightning. It snapped and popped with arcs of electricity in between my palms. This would be enough to nearly kill a human. But, it merely tickled me. With a good deal of concentration, I pulled the lightning back within me and focused on the storm of power inside of me.

I'd done this a lot over the last months. Since my turning, there had been a great disturbance in the force. Okay yes, I know, a quote from *Star Wars*, but that's how it felt. I felt like the power I held when I was a witch was only a fraction compared to the well of power that was in me now. This amount of power had proven to be difficult to tame. As if one really could tame lightning. I repeated this practice for hours. I barely noticed when Mark returned for the dishes and to drop off my dinner.

He eyed me with caution when he saw what I was doing.

I sighed and said while pulling my power to one hand, tossing the ball of lightning in the air and catching it, "You know, Mark, I really am a nice person. I have been forced into a situation I can do nothing about. And the man I love is gone. Being kept somewhere." I stopped tossing the ball of lightning and pulled it back into me, feeling it settle deep within my core. I walked over to him and he tensed as though he just knew I would lay his ass out.

"How would you feel, Mark? How would you feel if Mitch had done this to your female?"

I took the plates from him and set them on the edge of the bed and turned to face him. He stood there thinking. And that shocked the hell out of me. He genuinely was thinking about my words.

He met my eyes and just before he looked away he said in a low tone, "I would fight at every turn."

He turned and walked out. I stood there gaping for the second time today. I now had one week until the new moon when I would be at my weakest, but so would all the other wolves. That would be the best time for me to try anything to get out of here. I had a good feeling about this, this time. Mark was my ticket out of here. Now, I just had to figure out how to make him play ball. I was sick of feeling sorry for myself. I wanted out of this miserable situation. So, I had to get myself out. Then I needed to find Reid. I was not the damsel in this story and I would never be. Time to pull up the big girl panties and save my own ass.

RiED JAMiSON

TWO

THE DEPRESSION I *feel is so overwhelming, I think it may swallow me whole.*

My heart hurt.

Maybe it's not even a heart anymore, maybe it's just a huge gaping hole with nothing there.

I'd never been a man who expressed emotion or feelings in an outward manner, but these emotions and pure self-loathing were crippling. I closed my eyes and all I could see was her. Her blood-spattered white dress. Her mangled neck. She'd said, "I love you." And I tried to rage and roar to save her. In the end, all I accomplished was not being able to tell her I loved her back.

Had I done this? Had I set all of these events in motion? Had I not protected her? In the last four months, I'd asked myself these questions over and over again. I always went back and forth on the answers. My mind had started playing tricks on me. I had no idea how long I'd been locked in this cage, but it had started to affect how I saw things. Was she even real? Had she ever touched me? Kissed me? My thoughts and memories began to blur together in some kind of marriage. I often saw her. I saw her silhouette and like always when I saw her, she was out of my reach. And the moment I did find her, her form became insubstantial for it was always non-corporeal.

Seeing her die, then seeing her form and never being able to touch her was maddening. I was losing control of my thoughts and I knew it. God, the dreams. I would wake up from the dreams crazed and murderous. The guards feared me, as they should. That didn't stop them from taunting me though. I tried to get information from them for four months and had achieved not one bit of it. They wouldn't even tell me if she rose or not.

I'd not seen Mitch since the night he killed Delaney. Even thinking her name and his name in the same thought made me wretch what little bile I had left in my stomach. So, when I caught his scent, it shocked me so hard that the fragile grip I held on the beast that lived inside of me almost slipped. I could smell him, but not her. Then I heard footsteps. Slow, sure footfalls. Then the whistling began. I knew the tune. *Save the Last Dance for Me* by the Drifters. I snarled, partly because I couldn't help it, but mainly because the song was rather apropos.

The whistling grew louder and more insistent. I began growling so deep in my chest that I could feel the vibrations against my skin. Then I saw him. The bomb detonated at the sight of his smug smile. I charged the silver bars. I did little to them, as I expected. He flinched. The motion was imperceptible, but it was there. I smiled.

"Tisk-tisk-tisk, is that any way to greet me? Gosh, the high and mighty Reid Jamison, how you have fallen."

"What do you want, you glorified piece of shit?" My voice was raw from my constant yelling. I would use every bit of energy I had to not show an ounce of weakness in front of this male.

"Aww, you wound me," he said, clutching the place on his chest where his heart should have been.

"What do you want?" I could hear the resignation in my own voice and it disgusted me.

He smiled with all teeth and said, "My guards tell me you're becoming irate and asking after Delaney. I thought I would bring you a little information."

I narrowed my eyes at him. *Why would he give me anything? But, I did wonder why he kept me this long and why he had yet to kill me.* Despite my misgivings about anything this man would tell me, my heartbeat kicked into high gear at her name.

"Let's see … What should I tell you?" He tapped his finger against his lips in mock thought. Then, seeming to have an idea, he pointed that finger up to the sky and said, "Oh, I know! Did you know that when she comes, her whole body vibrates with an electrical current? Every. Inch. Of. Her."

My vision went completely red and I charged the bars. Because every word he spoke was true, but there was a lie in it. He may know that about her, but I couldn't believe he'd had her. Never. Not like that. Unless he forced her. I had to hold on to that thought or I would grow mad. Then, I saw something white poking out of his suit sleeve. I froze, recognizing it. It looked to be a bandage. I smiled up at him. Then I started laughing in a way that only madmen did. His eyes narrowed this time.

"Oh, Mitch, I love how you come here and try to convince me you have been with her. All you have done is proven to me that she is indeed alive and she's been fighting you at every turn. Looks like she got you pretty good on your arm. Thanks for the visit and chit-chat. Really, Mitch, it has been illuminating."

It was he who charged the bars this time. And, at that moment, I knew I was right. She was alive and she had fought him. *Oh, thank goodness my girl is fighting him*. Both thoughts eased the out-of-control storm that was sitting beneath my skin. It soothed the beast. He seemed to catch himself at that moment and stop himself from rattling my cage even more. His upper hand was slipping and my beast, not to mention his, knew it. *Now, if these bars were not standing between us, this conversation would have had a different ending*.

He smoothed a hand over his hair, fixing the bits that had fallen out of place. He had on a navy-blue fitted suit, a skinny silver tie with a white button-down shirt, and black shoes. He was dressed to impress, though it did little to affect me. I looked down at myself. I was covered in dirt, caked-on sweat and grime. I hadn't a stitch of clothing on. My hair was a matted mess, as was my growing beard.

"Why, Mitch, are we going on a date? You're so dressed up. God, and I didn't bring anything to wear," I quipped in my best needling tone, but it just came out as me being a prick. I shrugged.

"Reid, you forget I have her. And it's a matter of time. She will become my mate and there will be little you can do about that," he responded while fiddling with the French cuffs on his shirt sleeves.

"Why do you want her? I mean yes, you have proven this prophecy to be true. Why is possessing her so important?"

"You have not been given the whole prophecy, Reid. I need her to take down the witches. And then we will have control over the supernatural world. Then, we will force the weres out in public and it will only be a matter of time before we gain control of everything."

"Really, that seems like a lofty goal," I scoffed. Frankly, it seemed a bit out there.

"Not when we have spent the last few years getting weres into high-level government positions." He was so sure of himself and his tone only mirrored his self-confidence.

Then the full impact of what he was saying hit me. From moment one, he was planning this takeover. If he truly had wolves in these positions, he could very well do as he was saying. It just seemed off for what I knew of him, or what I thought I knew. He was selfish; he couldn't give a single fuck about other weres.

"Why are you keeping me alive?" The meaning of the word alive was living, and this was not living. But, I had to call this existence something.

"Delaney refuses to change without an updated picture of you. And I use you to control her. It's that simple." He walked over to the stairs that led to the exit. He turned to me and smiled.

"She is soft, you know? Her curves are supple, and her warm little mouth is so hungry. I think I'll get back to my little white wolf."

I charged the bars snarling at him, but he was gone.

I paced around the cell for hours after Mitch left. I had no real plan or even thoughts, other than of her. Just knowing she was fighting him sent a surge of hope through me. I wasn't sure why it was making me feel hopeful, but for the first time in months, I felt something other than pain and depression.

I had no windows in this small dank cell, but the light that illuminated under the door at the top of the cell went from natural to fluorescent, so I could tell that it was night. Being in this cell day in and day out played tricks on my mind. So, when I felt as though I had no recollection of the time of day, I would focus on the only source of light to help keep myself grounded.

I walked over to the small cot and fell on it. Maybe my dreams would be of her. Maybe now that I knew my love was alive and fighting, it would help strengthen my resolve and I would find the will to get the hell out of here and find her. I raised my arms, tucked them under my head, and drifted for a while in memories of Delaney, before succumbing to mental exhaustion.

HER SKIN FELT like heated satin. I slipped my hands from her hair, down her shoulders to her plump breasts. She liked when I did this. I cupped both of the soft mounds and began to knead them with the same wicked rhythm she was grinding on me. Oh, gods, she was rubbing her drenched sex along the length of my cock, but she refused to put me fully inside of her. This was her game and it was maddening.

I leaned up and licked the tight little bud of her nipple. She moaned with each lap of my tongue. I licked, but never sucked her into my mouth. It was driving her crazy each time my tongue touched her, and she arched to me, seeking more. With my other hand, I rolled her pink little-pebbled flesh between my finger and thumb. She never eased her maddening grind on my now pulsing cock. And at that point, she was so wet I could slip so easily inside of her. I was being driven to the brink. If this went on much longer, I would spill without even burying myself inside of her.

I finally sucked her nipple inside my mouth and she cried out in pleasure. Oh, now I was going to explode.

"Delaney, I need to be inside of you. Now." It was a snarl, but I didn't care. She shifted and I could feel myself at her entrance. I stilled, letting her take me into her body. It took every bit of strength I had not to impale her on my throbbing cock. It was so slow. She eased down on top of me so tenderly it was driving me mad.

I could see her pulse pounding in her throat and a bead of sweat rolled down over the fluttering skin. I wanted to lick the trail it made. I leaned up and ran my tongue down its path and suckled at the frantically beating skin. I was fully in her and she was so tight and wet I nearly came at the first connection of feeling her like that.

Suddenly, she began screaming as though she were on fire. I drew my head back in a daze to see what happened. Her throat was a mangled mess of blood and gnarled meat. My eyes went wide in panic. She fell off of me, holding her neck, and the look in her eyes grew distant. They went white, the way a witch's did in death. I reached up to my mouth. It was wet. I brought up my damp hand to see her blood coating my mouth. Me. I'd done this to her.

I flew awake. My hands went immediately to my face. It was damp with sweat, nothing more. My heart was pounding in my chest. I closed my eyes trying to calm down, but all I saw was her on top of me with blood coating the front of her and her look of shock and betrayal. I opened my eyes to stare at the ceiling.

It was the same goddamn dream every fucking night. This confinement wouldn't drive me crazy, but these dreams sure would be the death of me. I lifted my head to peer over my body to see what time of day it was. The stairwell was dark. *Great, still night. More time for me to dream.* I did not want to dream so I got up off the cot and started doing pushups. When my arms began to burn, I switched to burpees. When my muscles began to quiver, I returned to the cot. Over the months, I'd learned if I was active I didn't dream of Delaney as much. Some sick part of me wanted to keep dreaming this dream. Even though it ended the same way every time, it was the only time I got to see her.

I felt myself drifting back to sleep and I would at least get to be with her there.

I TURNED AROUND. I was in Delaney's apartment? I made a circle, trying to figure out how I got there. Everything looked the same from the last time I was there. Even her beloved French press sat out on the counter with what looked to be coffee brewing in it. My heart raced at the thought. Could she be here? I ran through the small apartment and found it empty.

"Hello?" I called to the empty apartment.

"Hello, Reid," a voice with a slightly eastern European accent came from behind me. I didn't turn to face it, because I knew the voice all too well. A chill ran up my spine. Slowly, after I took a moment to dial down my aggression, I faced him.

"What are you doing here?" I questioned between gritted teeth.

"Oh, Reid, is that any way to greet your maker?" His tone was scolding.

"How did we get here?" I asked, eyeing the apartment.

"You picked this place, wolf. I am not surprised, because it was hers," he said, walking over to the French press. He got two coffee cups out and poured the hot liquid into them. The room was filled with the rich scent of the steaming brew. My heart ached because it reminded me of her.

"Who are you? I mean you changed me and I have a feeling you aren't just some prick werewolf going around changing people," I commented, eyeing him as he walked over to the table. He offered me a cup before he sat down. Was any of this real? I sipped the coffee and the heated liquid coated my tongue and slid down my throat, causing me to shudder in pleasure at the rich taste. It sure as hell tasted real.

He smiled at me. "I have many names. Taranucno, Taranuo, Taraino, and others." He drank deeply from his mug and eyed the liquid as though he was surprised at something. He met my eyes and continued, "Through history my name has changed, but Delaney's people and yours knew me as Taranis."

His name seemed to echo through the empty apartment. I eyed him warily.

"I'm not sure what those names mean. I still have no idea who you are other than the asshole who changed me."

Then something happened that sent fear, unlike anything I had ever felt before, through all of me. His image flickered, much like a hologram would. The being underneath his human image was a creature that looked to be made of nothing but lightning. That was when it clicked. This man. This being. This thing was a god. And I just called him an asshole. *Great job, Reid.* Now, he would strike me down for sure.

"Reid, this *asshole* is the whole reason you have her."

My eyes widened not just at his tone of such self-assurance, but at what he said.

"Why did you turn me?" This is a question I have held for many years and I made a vow that if I were to ever face the animal who did this to me, I would ask him. This would surely be one of the only chances I would ever get.

"Because my daughter needs you." His face softened marginally at the thought of Delaney.

Wait, his daughter? Delaney was the daughter of a god? The weight of that fact nearly sent me staggering back.

"Does she know? That you're parent to her?" It came out as more breath than words, but I was still reeling that the woman I loved was part god.

"No, but she will. She needs you, Reid. She needs you to be whole. She needs you to not let this break you, because, Reid, she is breaking."

"What do you mean she's breaking?" I asked, setting my cup down on the table. My voice was trembling. The thought of anything more happening to her, something that I couldn't be there to prevent, made me quake with madness and hurt.

"A person, even if they are of me, cannot go through so much loss and pain and still come out the other side unchanged," he explained, eyeing me. He seemed so unaffected by his words. I could imagine this would be the same tone he would order his dinner with.

"Then help her! Or get me out of here and I'll go get her!" I was losing my cool and I knew it. I grabbed the edge of the table, trying to steady myself and not lash out at a being that could surely kill me.

"I cannot. There is only so much I can do. You know, free will and all that you humans so love." There was an audible snap. I looked down to find the edge of the table broken and in pieces.

"So, why come here? Why tell me any of this if there is nothing I can do to help her?" I was speaking through clenched teeth. Damn it, if there was nothing I could do, why come at all?

He rubbed his chin in thought. The light that danced in his dark eyes dulled. He seemed to genuinely think about the question, almost as though he forgot why he was here. He snapped his fingers and life seemed to return to his eyes.

"I have something for you! And I have a word of advice," he nearly yelled as he stood up. I backed away from the table, not really wanting to get too close to him. I saw him shove his hand into his pocket and pull out a small gold coin. He handed it to me and I took it.

I looked up to see him, smiling at me. Okay, so now what?

"Okay, what do I do with this?" I mean, would it turn into a key to get me the hell out of my prison?

"You'll know what to do with it when you are in need of it."

Seriously? Just as I was about to question him further, something flashed across his face that led me to believe he wouldn't tell me more.

"Reid, haven't you found it odd that the amount of guards you see in a day has been reduced to two? Seems as though this pack is becoming … complacent," he asked as he walked to the door. He turned to face me and I stood there dumbfounded, because no, I hadn't noticed that. I'd had so much inner strife that I wouldn't have noticed anything.

"I hadn't," I admitted, not meeting his eyes.

"Reid, you have one week until the new moon. I need to you be there for my lightning bug." His words filled the apartment long after he walked out.

This god needed me to be there for her. *Needed me to save her.* I would no longer allow myself to wallow in self-pity. I had a job to do and my love to save. I walked over to the couch and lay down. I closed my eyes and remembered her while I waited to wake up.

DELANEY HAGEN

THREE

MARK DELIVERED EVERY meal for the next two days. I took every chance I had to talk to him. I actually started to like the creepy little rat and that surprised the hell out of me. He was due to bring me breakfast in about ten minutes. I had a plan and needed him to help me. I needed to see if he was receptive at all, so I thought I would start small. *I just hope it will work.* Mitch still wasn't back from whatever venture he was on. That was the longest he had been gone since I was turned ... that I could remember anyway. Thank God I didn't have to see his smug face. Sometimes, I wished I had a pie that I could smash into it. Well, if by pie I meant anvil, then yes. I smiled at the visual. I really was sick.

He knocked at the door three minutes before his normal time.

"Hey, Mark, come in," I called in a cheery tone. Well, as cheery as I could manage in this cell. *Fake it until you make it, right?*

"Hey, Delaney," he said, backing into the room with a cart.

"Would you mind setting it on the desk?" I replied, piling all of my dirty clothes on the bed.

"Yeah, no problem." He walked over to the small oak desk in the far corner of the room. I continued piling the massive amount of clothes onto the bed.

"What are you doing?" he asked, eyeing me. His gaze went from the pile to me and then his eyes went wide at what I was wearing. Or rather what I wasn't wearing. I had on a bra and tiny little boy-running-style shorts. He whirled, putting his back to me.

Now, that surprised me. Who knew the rat had some manners?

"God, Delaney! Put some clothes on!" His tone was rough, but embarrassed. I expected to smell lust, but this was truly unexpected.

"Sorry, uff …" I trailed off, trying to steady the mountain of clothes. "... Mitch always brings me new clothes, but he's been away and I have nothing that's clean."

He turned to face me. He eyed the large pile and had a look of panic flash across his face.

"Uh okay. I can't wash them," he said, sputtering the words out as though they were obstacles to even say.

I put my hands on my hips and narrowed my eyes at him. "Well, why not?" A clump of hair fell into my eyes and I blew it out of my line of sight. All while never taking my eyes off of Mark.

He ran his hand through his greasy hair and didn't meet my eyes.

"I-I don't know how. My wife always washes the clothes." He seemed ashamed by admitting this fact. I think I was just staring at him, blinking and open-mouthed. How, in however many years he had been on this Earth, had he never learned how to wash clothes? And he was married? Good Lord, who knew? I guessed there really was someone for everyone. That thought caused a pang of hurt to prick my heart. I swallowed, trying to bite back a cry of pain at missing Reid.

"Well, what should I do?" The words held some of the emotions I was feeling, but I covered it by pushing my hip out in defiance. Well, I think all I really managed was pissy teenager.

"I-I don't know. Mitch won't be back until tonight. I'll let you out so you can wash a load of laundry. I'll be in the condo, so you can't leave. Delaney, I mean it. Please don't do anything that will get either of us killed," he said, returning my hands on hip gesture.

I smiled at him, ran at him and threw my arms around him in thanks. It seemed to surprise him as his body went completely stiff at the sudden contact. Hell, I surprised myself. I leaned to his ear and whispered, "Thank you so much. This whole thing has been so awful. Thank you for doing the first nice thing for me since I was turned."

He softened at my words and even raised an arm to wrap it around me.

As though he realized just who he was touching, he recoiled from me with surprising speed. Clearly I smelled bad.

"You have one hour. Don't fuck it up. And don't tell anyone I let you do this," he said as he left the room. And when he left the room, the door was open. Even this little bit of freedom made my heart rate speed up.

I grabbed a double armload of clothes and headed out of the dank room. I had a list of things to do and only an hour to do them in.

I'd been through this condo before. In fact, Mitch showed me around my second month here. Then he tried like hell to sleep with me. After he realized, through my not-so-subtle nos, also known as me burning his testicles so badly I doubt he could grow hair on them ever again, he put me in my cell of a room.

I nearly ran to the laundry room and threw my clothes in the washer. Then, I did the one thing I was explicitly told not to do. I went to Mitch's office. I mean I never really did follow directions well. I turned the knob, only to find it locked. Shit! *How the hell do I get in there?* My eyes widened at a memory of the time I locked my bedroom door and I had to call Troy over to help me. He reached on the top of the door frame and felt around for a small key that resembled a small flat-head screwdriver.

"Girl, your momma must have never locked you out before. Everyone keeps these things here."

I reached for the top of the door frame and gritted my teeth. I could barely reach. I stood on tip-toes and felt around, and there was nothing. It had to be there though, or else all this stupid venture would get me would be clean clothes. I tried again and just as I was about to give up, my fingertips brushed something small. I had to jump, but I finally got it. I was shaking by the time I slipped the small piece of metal into the door knob. I took a deep breath and felt the key slip into the groove and turn. The door clicked open. I took a deep breath and walked in. I wish I could say I had this amazing plan that would surely work, but I didn't. I was flying by the seat of my pants.

The office was twice the size of my small bedroom and I immediately felt totally cheated. There was an L-shaped cherry desk along the left and back walls, opposite the door. I walked over to it and began rifling through each drawer. I tried to view each and every item, but I had little time so I know there were things left unseen.

I walked over to the other side of the desk and opened a large drawer. In it was my purse. I picked it up and realized it was the one I had the night I died. I didn't even remember what I had in it. I opened it to find the letter that Mil left me. My skin went cold. I didn't have time to read it, but I did note it was there. I slipped it back into the drawer to get at a later time. My heart was about to beat out of my chest. I flipped through his contact information located in a small address book. I went down the list trying to see if there was anyone I knew. Then it dawned on me: I could use the fucking phone!

I grabbed the small address book and scrambled to the cordless phone on the desk. Just as I reached for it, I pulled back. Who would I call? Who would come and get me? I plopped down on the computer chair. God, I had no one. I put my head into my hands and held my breath. I had no idea what I was trying to accomplish. My mind was at a breaking point and I knew it. I was crumbling and trying desperately to grapple for some kind of purchase, finding nothing but the rubble of what once was my life. I felt the little book slip from my hand and fall to the floor. I glanced at it when a name caught my eye. Monique Thomas. But, her name was under the Cs. I wiped my eyes with my palm. They weren't tears. My eyes were just sweating.

I fingered the entry and couldn't understand why her name would be listed under the Cs. Her number was an out-of-state number; I had no idea where it was from. My eyes slid to a small black filing cabinet to the right of the desk. I got up and crossed to it, opening the first drawer and going to the Cs. I didn't know any of the names and most of them did not start with C. *What the hell?* I couldn't understand why the crap all of these people were under the Cs. Then I saw a name I knew, Bernard Tailor. He was the leader of the Coven. Could it really be that easy? C is for Coven as in all of the inner circle? I picked up the file for Monique, then walked over to the desk and began looking through it.

She was from New Orleans, born and raised. She was an Earth witch. An incredibly powerful one at that. She was the newest addition to the inner circle. Her file went on about a lot of personal details. Then there were pictures, intimate pictures that one only got if the person trusted you. Mitch was even in some of them. This had to be how he found out about the prophecy. Had she told him? *Oh, hell no.* My faced heated with rage. How could she? I narrowed my eyes at the black book with her phone number in it. I smiled. Well, how about I give my fellow witch a little call?

I picked up the phone and dialed her number. With each ring my rage built. And with my increasing anger, my erratic heartbeat picked up into a faster rhythm. I tried to formulate just what I would say when she …

"Hello?" Her voice cut through my thoughts like a knife. She had a slight Creole accent. She sounded young. Like me. I tried to hold onto my rage and ire.

"Hello? Is anyone there?"

I shook my head and tried to say something, anything.

"Hi, um, hello." *Really, Delaney? The woman who sold out one of her own kind and you say hello?*

"Hi. May I ask who this is?"

"Um, my name is Delaney, and-and ..." I felt tears prick my eyes. Damnit, I wouldn't be a sniffling twit.

"Oh, gods, Delaney! Reid told me about you. Are you *okay*?" Her tone turned frantic.

"He-he did?" I was confused. This was not at all how I thought this conversation would go.

"Delaney, is Reid not with you? God, I'm so sorry. I never meant for Mitch to know anything. He overheard a conversation. Wait, are you okay?" My head was reeling with her rambling.

"No." It was a whisper of a word. My throat was closing and I had to choke the words out, "I-I'm not okay." I felt a tear track down my cheek.

"God, Delaney, did Mitch ...?" Her words sounded as though they were ripped from her.

"He killed me. And then I ..." I bit my lower lip trying desperately not to break out in sobs.

"Oh no. I ..." I could hear the emotion in her words. She was pained. All of the rage and ire fell away. This would be the only time I had and she didn't seem like the stories I heard of the Coven. I took a deep measured breath and found a little starch and injected it in my spine.

"Monique, Mitch has me and I don't know how much longer I have before I break."

My words filled the small room, making the air around me feel heavy with foreboding. Or I was losing it, which was highly possible.

"Delaney, listen to me. The Coven is after you as well. They don't know what has happened and I won't tell them, but you need to get away. They started this ... program. A breeding program. They are trying to breed as many witches as possible. But, they are forcibly breeding the most powerful ones. If they find you, Delaney, they will try to …" She trailed off in what I assumed was her trying to gather her thoughts.

"Listen, get away and call me when you can, I'll help you if I …"

With a click the line went dead. I looked down at the phone. *What the hell was wrong with this thing?* I then looked up to find Mitch holding the cord of the phone in his hand.

My heart dropped out from under me. I knew it was coming, but when he rushed me, lifting me out of the chair by my hair, the pain knocked the breath out of me. He dragged me to the nearest wall and flattened me to it. I gritted my teeth at the pain. I tried to pull on my power, but he had to have felt it building, because he slammed my head against the wall again. My vision blurred at the impact. He flipped me so that I was facing the wall. As soon as he had me fully pressed against the flat surface, he took my hands and wrenched them behind my back, causing me to arch toward him. I screamed out in pain. My heart was a jackhammer in my chest.

"Was it worth it?" he snarled in my ear. I could feel his spittle misting me. I began pulling the lightning from my core again. I had to fight back. He felt my body tense and shifted my hands to one of his, then grabbed my hair again and ground my face into the wall.

"Do it, Delaney. Make this so much worse for yourself." His voice was guttural and I knew he was fighting his beast.

He then ground his pelvis into my lower back and I could feel his straining erection. God, he was getting turned on by this. *What a sick fuck.*

"Did Mark let you out?" His words were so garbled it took me a second to understand what he said. I had two choices. I could tell him the truth and get what could be the only person who might help me, and that was a huge might, killed. Or take whatever this punishment was and lie. My thoughts shifted to the moment Mark mentioned he had a wife. My mind was made up. I wouldn't be the one who took him away from her. I had no idea why, even after everything, I felt the need to be kind to him, but dammit, it was who I was, deep down buried under all of the rubble.

He ground into me harder and wrenched my hands farther. I could no longer hold in my cries of pain. I screamed.

"No! I got out myself. He did my laundry and had no idea I was even out."

I nearly screamed the words through clenched teeth. That admission only seemed to enrage him further.

"Oh, Delaney, that's a shame. But I'm happy. Now, we get to go play in my bedroom. And if you're a good girl, I'll lick your wounds when I'm done with you."

I felt a small prick on the side of my neck. The world went hazy. Where had that come from? Maybe he had it up his ass. I giggled. Everything faded to black.

SWIRLING LIGHTS. THE movement made me feel like I was about to lose my breakfast. The lights stopped swaying, but they were still a bit fuzzy around the edges. Where was I? I blinked, trying to clear my vision. My eyelids were like sandpaper. I tried to rub them, but my arms were strapped down something. And I was cold.

I heard a voice. It was tinny, or maybe far away. I couldn't make out what was being said, but whoever it was, was mad as hell. I felt a slap across my face and, like a light switch, the fog lifted and I saw Mitch. He was taking his white button-down shirt off. I was hanging by my wrists to chains that were fixed to his ceiling. I could stand only on my tip-toes.

"Mitch, please. I won't do it again," I lied.

He smiled at me, all teeth. He walked over to me and I felt my nipples brush his warm chest. I belatedly realized that I was cold because I had no clothes on. *Oh God*. I began to tremble with fear.

"Oh, Delaney. The only way you'll be getting out of this is if you offer yourself to me," he said, a mere inch away from my lips.

"Mitch," My voice was raspy. "You can go fuck yourself."

Just because I was in this position wouldn't mean I would give myself up to him.

Pain exploded from my jaw. My vision went black from the impact. It was only a moment, but holy hell, it hurt. I spat blood out that tasted extremely metallic. I waited for the pain to ebb, but it didn't. It throbbed with each of my frantic heart beats.

"Oh, is the little wolf not healing? That little shot was a mix to knock you out, but I slipped a little silver in there to slow your healing," he said, rubbing his balled fist. "I want you to feel everything that's about to happen to you now, and I want you to feel it tomorrow."

His words sent a shiver up my spine. I had no idea what he would do to me. But, I had to hold on as long as I could.

His blows rained down on me with the force of a hurricane. One after another. I heard and felt bones breaking. I tried like mad to pull my lightning out and strike back at him, but with my hands bound and the pain I was in, I couldn't hold onto the power for longer than a moment. After nearly every blow, he would run a rough hand over my body and ask if I was ready to accept him. And each time he asked this, I spat a single word. *Never.* I knew if I pushed him much further he would force himself on me. But I would never give myself to him. Never. Each time I said no it only enraged him more. I passed out countless times. Sometimes, I would come to only to be assaulted once again by his fists or knees. Other times I came to with his mouth on me. At some point I couldn't hold back the tears.

After hours of pain and torture, he took me down from the chains. I couldn't stand on my own. He threw me on his bed, kicked my legs open wide. I yelled and screamed. *No, no this can't be happening.* But I found I had little strength to fight him. I used what little voice I had left. It was all I had. And, as though he finally heard me, he roared in frustration. He walked out of the room. I was in shock. *Maybe, he had a moment of kindness?* The thought was ridiculous. I was far from caring why he stopped, I was just glad I had this small reprieve. I wanted to run, shit I wanted to run. The door opened and I tensed. But, it wasn't Mitch, I scented Mark? It was so hard to tell from the scent of my own blood.

I felt his hands slip under me. Then another scent hit me. Rage. And it was Mark's. *God, why is Mark pissed?* He lifted me in his arms and cradled me to his chest.

"God, Delaney. You should have just told him I let you out." His voice was low and barely a whisper.

I opened my mouth to speak, but my jaw wouldn't move. My vision was red with my blood.

"Shhh, don't try to speak. God damn him. He has gone too far this time." I felt him lay me down on something soft. He smoothed a hand over my bloody forehead.

"Mark!" Mitch's voice called from the hallway.

Mark left and, for the first time, I felt his absence as a physical and emotional loss. I coughed, trying to clear my damaged lungs.

"I'll be gone for a few days. But I'll be back for the new moon. Impress upon her that this is her last chance before I take what I need," he spat the words.

"Yes, sir." Mark's voice was low.

"And, Mark," I heard what I thought was Mitch hitting him, and Mark's breath leave him with a whoosh. "Don't let something like this happen again. Or it won't be your head, it will be Kate's."

I could no longer fight it. I closed my eyes and let darkness overwhelm me.

REiD JAMiSON
FOUR

TOMORROW NIGHT WAS the night of the
new moon. I could feel my power and strength waning
just as the moon began its draining pull. I would be at
my weakest, but then so would whoever was guarding
me. Tomorrow night was to be the night I would get
out of this hell hole. But, I still had no idea how this
coin would aid me in my escape. I fully understood
that there would be only two guards here if the god
was correct. I had never tried to get out, so they had
grown complacent. Damn it, even MacGyver had more
than a fucking coin to get himself out of a damn bind.

Maybe I just wasn't thinking outside the box.
Maybe I could bend the coin in the form of a key and

… okay, that was the dumbest thought I may have ever had. A key out of a coin? I paced the length of the cell and tried to think of what to do with the damn coin.

A bribe? The coin appeared to be made of gold. But, with the long lives we had, money meant nothing to some of the older wolves. I flipped the coin up in my hand as I walked. Then I paused to look at it. Maybe there were directions, like shove into eye socket of enemy. No such luck. On one side, there was a wheel of some kind. Not as in a circle, but much like a wagon wheel with spokes. The other side was the head of a wolf.

I rubbed my thumb over the etching and the wolf's depiction disappeared. My eyes widened and I ran my thumb over the carving again. The depiction of the wolf's head was once again on the coin. I flipped the small disk to the side with the wheel and ran my thumb over the surface. Nothing happened. Had I imagined it? I flipped the coin once more and ran my thumb over the top of it. Once again, the wolf head was gone. And when I did it again, the head reappeared.

Just then, I heard the door at the top of the stairs open. I looked at the light spilling through the stairwell. With the amount of light showing, I would guess it was noon. Lunch time. I caught the scent of the wolf coming down the stairs and it made me smile.

Phil wasn't a new wolf to Mitch's pack, but he also was not high up in the pecking order. Phil was a short African American man who was turned when he was just shy of twenty-one or so. He had been turned about fifteen years ago. He had a nearly shaved head and muscular build. I think, before he was changed, he was training as an amateur bodybuilder. He, like most of the pack, worshiped Mitch. The sun rose and set by Mitch according to his pack, but especially Phil. He was also the one I could goad into giving me information just by pissing him off. I still needed some information before I could get the hell out of dodge. Like, where the hell were we? Where was Delaney being held? And why? Why any of this? What was his ultimate goal?

I realized I still held the coin. I walked over to the cot and shoved it under the blanket to try to hide its presence. I looked up to see Phil standing at the entrance to the cell, fumbling with the tray and keys.

"Oh, look, it's Mitch's lap dog," I spat.

He gave a low growl, but wouldn't speak to me. They were told not to converse with me. Though, this man did, if I could anger him enough to do it.

"Or should I say Mitch's little bitch? Does he mount you like a little …?"

He snarled and yelled, "Shut up!" He continued to fumble with the keys. He was trying to get the key into the slot at this point. I could just rush him, but I would need someone to open the gate at the top of the stairs. I highly doubted that the other guard would let me out even if he saw his pack mate in trouble. I needed to bide my time and wait for tomorrow. The god in my dream told me to leave on the new moon and I would.

"You know, Phil," I spat his name as though it were a cuss word, "you're a smart guy, really you are. So, what I don't get is why you're in this."

Phil's mounting frustration boiled over. He dropped my tray with a solid smack. He then shoved the key in the lock. He briskly turned the key, pulled the door open, and kicked the tray in. The tray slid across the cell floor until it smacked into the back wall with a thud. He slammed the cell door and then narrowed his eyes at me.

"Mitch is my alpha and moreover, he's right. We have spent too many years in hiding. Too many years pretending we are humans. We have let the Coven shove us under a rock. It's time that they end and it's time that we start anew. Why can't you see that?" He sounded like a zealot, like he believed every single word that fell from his lips.

"Oh, I don't know, it could be because your high and mighty leader killed the woman I love. And then he has kept me locked in this cell for nearly four months, barely allowing me to change and run." At my words, a shiver wracked his body. Not changing into our wolf selves would become painful after a time and if we couldn't change, the wolf inside us would find a way to claw its way out and we would likely never be able to gain the upper hand again. While I have been able to change, I was not allowed to run or hunt. This was denying the wolf in me part of itself. At least he was not unfeeling about the situation.

He met my eyes and said in a measured tone, "They are necessary losses."

"Would you sacrifice your female? And give up all you have for this ..." I scoffed, "... cause?"

He walked to the bars and tossed me a scrap of material.

"Put these on. I'm sick of seeing you naked."

"Jealous?" I said smugly.

He walked to the stairs, and I called to his back, "You never answered me." He never looked back at me. He rapped on the door for the other guard to let him out. His non-answer was answer enough. I heard him pause at the top of the stairs.

"You know Reid, you might want to be a little more pleasant. Mitch promised that after he had Delaney, we all get a turn with the bitch. I think I'll have my turn recorded for you." The door shut behind him, cutting off any response I had. I gritted my teeth.

Like fuck you will, asshole. You aren't going to live that long. And for saying that, I'll make sure it's painful.

I learned little from him, but I did notice one small detail. The athletic shorts he tossed at me not only smelled of him, but of snow. We weren't in the south anymore. I had a long way to travel to get to her. I *would* get to her, even if all I had to do it with was a coin.

I RUBBED MY thumb over the coin, causing the etching to disappear and reappear. What the hell could it mean? How could this coin help me get out of this prison? I spent all night trying to dream of the god in hopes of questioning him further, but the only dream I had was the same one I'd been plagued with since Delaney died. Needless to say, I did not sleep much at all. The new moon was already at its highest point, and there I sat, flipping a coin and trying desperately to figure out how to get out of here. I tried to think back to my knowledge of this god. Really, what did I know about him?

Taranis was worshiped by the Celts prior to the first and second centuries BCE. Sadly, that was all the information I knew. Delaney said from the information she had gathered from her Aunt Mil, that both of our species were once one being, the Druid. Because the act of human sacrifices were outlawed, the tithes the Druids owed to the gods were not paid, thus it created a rift in the power base and the powers split. Now there were witches and werewolves. *There has got to be something I'm missing.* Did the Druids have other powers that they lost in the split? This not knowing, and not having a way to know, was maddening. If only I had a way to find out!

I threw the damn thing in frustration. The small gold coin bounced along the cement, floor sparking once and then bouncing against the adjacent wall. At the same moment the coin sparked, lightning struck just outside. The cracking boom was nearly deafening. My hands flew to my ears. Was it raining? Or had the coin done that? No, that's crazy. I got up from the cot and walked over to the coin. I eyed it in my hand. Again, I tossed the small disk. Again the coin sparked against the ground and again I heard the loud crack of lightning striking just outside the cell. The force of the strike was so powerful that the wall of the cell cracked, and I felt the heat of it through the cement blocks. My eyes widened in shock. I picked up the coin and smiled at it.

I looked up to the ceiling and said, "Talk about bringing the house down."

I walked over to the bars and tried to quiet my frantic heartbeat enough to listen for any stirring from the guards. After a while, I only heard the dull thrum of a TV playing somewhere in the upper level. I glanced down at the coin and realized that two of the eight spokes that were on the wheel were gone. *Great, this limits the use of the coin.* I walked over to the cot and sat atop it. I wondered if the force of the strike had anything to do with the force of the lightning.

I threw the coin, fairly hard, at about a 45-degree angle. It bounced once with a bright spark before it hit the adjacent wall and then it sparked again with the second impact. With each spark, there was a strike of lightning, and with both bolts the crack in the wall not only became larger, but smaller cracks began to branch off. Much like a crack in glass, each strike had other smaller cracks that splintered off of it, weakening the structure as a whole. Small rocks and fine dust began to fall from the abrasions. I retrieved the coin and looked at the wheel. It now only had four spokes left. I felt a bead of sweat roll down my forehead. My heart was nearly beating through my chest. I heard the door at the top of the stairs open with a sad groan. I ran over to the coin and slipped it into my pocket. I placed my back so that it was covering the bulk of the crack.

Only seconds later did I see Phil's face peering at me. He held a dinner tray. I let out a breath I'd not realized I was holding. He walked over to the cell door and this time he set the tray down before dealing with the keys. The door gave way with a loud squeal of protest. He kicked the tray in and shut the cell door. All without saying a word.

"That's some storm we're having," I said in a casual tone.

"Yeah, kind of came out of nowhere," he said, ascending the stairs.

I paused for a long moment. About thirty seconds later, I heard whatever show he was watching resume its dull thrum.

I walked over to the cot and moved it until it was sitting parallel with the back wall. I then stepped back until I felt the cool concrete against my bare back. I reached back with the coin in my hand and threw it at the same angle as before. This time I threw it as hard as

I could. I was rewarded with a spark so bright that I needed to shield my sensitive eyes. The lightning strike would have sent me staggering had my back not been against a wall. The wall cracked straight through. I could smell the scent of ozone, growing things and fresh snow. I gritted my teeth at the thoughts of Delaney that the scent of ozone brought.

I retrieved the coin and repeated the action two more times. With each lightning strike, the cracks in the wall grew larger. There was one spoke on the wheel left. This would be my last chance. I reached back and let loose the coin with all of the force that I could muster. The crack of the lightning strike caused me to go deaf. I couldn't hear anything for a solid five seconds. I shook my head as if that would do any good. I looked over to the wall. My heart sank to see it still standing. I walked over and rested my forehead against the cracked surface. What had I done wrong? I hadn't come this far to have her just out of my reach! I punched the wall in frustration. A small portion of the wall gave way. *Oh hell. Hitting things? Oh, this I could do.*

I swiftly snatched up the coin and rubbed my thumb over the wolf's head, causing it to disappear. I still had no idea what that did, but I had little time to contemplate it. I shoved the metal into my pocket. I began my assault on the damn wall. With every punch, I not only felt the wall give a little more, but dust and small bits of rubble rained down to the ground. This wall stood between Delaney and me. God, what I wouldn't do to get to her. I would bring down a thousand walls, a thousand armies, a thousand Covens. I would wait a thousand years, and in the end, I would still need her to breathe. My heart beat stronger because she filled it. She was my mate, and I knew it.

I was covered in sweat by the time I heard the structure groan and a five-foot-by-three-foot section of the wall crumbled to the floor. The door at the top of the stairs was wrenched open, and both guards nearly fell down them. I could have run. But I needed to make these men pay, if not with their lives then they needed to pay with their pain. When they reached the cell their eyes widened at the gaping hole in the wall. Their eyes searched the cell, but they never stopped on me.

"Oh fuck! He's gone!" Phil said, nearing on hysterics.

Gone? I'm standing right here. His eyes were darting from one end of the cell to the other. With each passing second, he grew more frantic. He opened the cell door and darted in with the other guard close on his heels. They both rushed right past me. I whirled to face them. They acted as though I weren't here at all. I couldn't figure it out.

"Oh God, he is going to kill us! Phil, what, what do we do?" This guard was tall and lanky. He had jet-black hair with eyes that nearly matched it. He stood about six feet tall. I had no idea of his name because this was the first time I'd seen him.

"Jose, I don't fucking know," Phil said in a panicked tone. I circled them as they looked at the cell in confusion. Then the memory of the coin flashed in my head. *Oh shit. Tricky tricky, god.* It did strike me as odd that they couldn't scent I was still in the room. These men were much younger than I and were most likely disregarding what their noses were telling them because it contradicted with what their eyes were seeing.

I circled around the pair until I stood directly behind Jose. I could kill him so easily. The decision was made when Phil said, "Jose, we have to let Mitch know. Call him." Jose pulled his cell phone out of his pocket. Without thought, I raised my hands to his head. With one quick jerk, there was an audible snap of bone. He crumpled to the floor like a rag doll. It wouldn't kill him, but it would take him several hours to regain consciousness and then a day for the injury to heal. In the end, I decided to let him live. But Phil, his fate was sealed.

Phil's gaze went wide and he took a few steps back. His eyes went wild. Then a sweet scent assaulted my nose. The beast inside stirred. My mouth watered. Fear. That scent sent a shiver up my spine. I was excited by it. I rushed him, grabbing him by his throat. I slammed him against the wall. His head cracked with the impact. His feet dangled just above the floor. I shoved my left hand into my pocket and rubbed the face of the coin. Phil would have screamed in shock had I not been crushing his windpipe. One of my now claws punctured the side of his neck. The scent of his blood mixed with his fear was enough to nearly turn me. I held onto my control, but only just. I knew my eyes were fully glowing green at this point.

"Oh, Phil, you seem to be in a bit of a bind," I said in a guttural tone. My voice had become raw and deep. I was holding on to get these words out.

His mouth opened to say something, but I squeezed his throat tighter. His mouth only gaped. His expression, with his eyes bugging out and his mouth gaping, reminded me of a goldfish out of water.

"I would have you tell Mitch I'm coming. There are no words for what I'm going to do to him. There will be a new category just to explain what I'll do to him. But, Phil, you need to be an example."

The words were barely audible due to the gravel in my voice.

Phil worked his jaw as though to say something. I loosened my grasp on him slightly.

In a bare whisper he rasped, "It won't save her." My vision went red, and I snapped his pitiful neck. I didn't stop at that small of an injury. I gripped him, and my muscles bunched and flexed as I worked them. I pulled with every bit of strength I had. I felt the moment his skin, bones, tendons, and muscles gave way. I didn't often use my supernatural strength like this. I felt the warm spray of blood coat my chest and abdomen. The metallic tang of it filled the air, and again my mouth watered. His body crumpled in a heap to the floor. I dropped his detached head and it made a wet thudding noise upon impact. I eyed the other man lying on the ground. I bent down and snatched up his body, and did the same thing to him. Mitch was now two down from his pack. I'd thought about letting the guard live, but that would only prove how weak I was. I turned my back from the gruesome scene and stepped through the hole.

The dark landscape was coated with a white blanket of snow. There were no lights, so the shadows of the rolling hills seemed to create an eerie painting. I thought about getting the keys off of Phil and driving out of here, but knowing Mitch, he likely had trackers on those damn things. With my mind made up, I slipped my shorts off and balled them up so that the coin wouldn't slip out. I took a deep breath of cold fresh air and then began my shift into my other self. My skin was set aflame by the burn of the change coupled with the burning cold. This shift was agonizing with the moon being new. I gritted my teeth and pushed harder. Finally, after about six minutes, I was fully changed. I padded over to my shorts and picked them up with my teeth.

Without looking back, I ran. I needed to find something to orient myself. So I let the beast out and let go. I knew he would find his mate. I knew I would find Delaney. Now, it was just a matter of when.

DELANEY HAGEN

FiVE

"DELANEY, WHY DIDN'T you just tell him I let you out?" Mark questioned as he wiped a damp rag over my eyes.

I was caked in dried blood. I tried to be strong. But I still couldn't stifle a wince at his touch. After a moment, he cleared the dried blood enough so I could see.

"Your wife," I rasped. My throat was dry and gods, everything hurt. I felt like I'd been hit by a truck. Then the asshat driving backed up and hit me a few more times for good measure. Mark stiffened at my words.

"I didn't want her to lose you, because Mitch would have killed you." My voice was still raspy, but it was feeling better.

Mark placed a straw in my mouth and I sucked in the cool liquid. Water. God, had anything ever tasted better than this? I drank deeply. Mark took the straw out of my mouth before I was done.

"Take it easy, go slow or you'll make yourself sick," he scolded. I tried to get up, but Mark put a hand on my shoulder and pressed me back down to the bed. "Stop. Look, you're healing, but with the injection he gave you, it will take you a few more hours. You have a few more ribs that need to heal." His tone was pointed.

Did he feel sympathy? Did it matter? I wasn't getting out of here. I squeezed my eyes tight, trying to keep my wild emotions in check, but I felt my heated tears roll down my cheeks. Then I felt Mark's warm touch brush them away. I cracked my eyes and tried to read his face. He still had the pained expression in his eyes. Or, at least, I thought he did. It was hard to tell through the tears flooding my vision.

"Why are you here, Mark?" Really, what I wanted to ask was, "Why do you care?"

"No one has ever protected me or my wife like you did. I have given you no reason to, but you did it anyway." He looked away as he spoke, as though it pained him further to look at me.

"Please, help me sit up." I wanted to not feel so helpless. Through much grumbling, he did as I asked. God, why did I feel so drained?

"How long was I out?" I questioned.

"A few days. It's the new moon tonight." *Shit.* I let out a breath. Why did I care? I knew I would never get out of here. Eventually I knew Mitch would get what he wanted, despite how much I fought him. My will was broken. Everything was broken. My heart hurt as though it would never beat again. Mark must have seen the defeat in my eyes.

"Look," he said, scooting closer to me and glancing back at the door. In a lower tone he whispered, "I'm going to do what I can to help get you out of here."

My eyes widened, but then fell. What could he do? Short of killing Mitch, there was nothing we could do. He would come after me. *God, how I want to kill him.*

But I couldn't. He was the one who turned me; I was physically unable to do it, as was Mark.

"How do you say we do that? Because the way I see it, Mitch is going to beat the living shit out of me until I give up and go to his bed. Or he's going to force himself on me. Either way I'm not getting out of here."

God, even my words made my stomach turn in disgust with myself. I felt irrevocably broken.

"Rest. I have a plan. You'll have to trust me though. I'll come back when I bring your dinner and I'll let you in on the plan. For now, you need to heal the rest of the way," he said, giving my shoulder a squeeze.

Could I trust him? I don't see how I have any other choice.

"I'm taking a shower, then I'll get back in bed."

He nodded and stood up to leave.

"Mark?"

He turned to face me.

"If whatever you have planned fails, thank you."

He nodded and without a word, he left and locked the locks on the door.

I thought getting out of the warm bed would be the hard part. Oh no, walking was the hard part.

Apparently, the bastard truck driver ran me over more times than I thought. After about an hour of shambling, I made it to the small bathroom. I swear zombies were faster than me. I turned the shower on and waited for the water to heat.

I undressed and stepped in. The heated water on my skin felt like needles at first, but soon it eased some of the built-up tension. My thoughts slid to Mitch. The things he had done to me, not just the beating, the other things. I wanted him to suffer in the same ways. I pictured slowly cutting off his head. *Oh God, Delaney, what are you letting him turn you into?* This was not me. I was happy. I was goofy. I felt like Mitch was slowly killing me from the inside out. Maybe I was becoming a cold, unfeeling monster just like him.

I stood under the shower until the water ran cold. I dressed and then got into bed. At least this time I could stand a fighting chance against the undead. Maybe if I were up against zombies, I would die second, not first.

I could feel myself healing. If whatever Mark had planned did work, I would have to find out where they were keeping Reid and get him. I closed my eyes, hoping to slip into a dreamless healing sleep. For some reason I had a strange feeling it wouldn't be that easy.

OUCH. OUCH. SHIT. I swatted at my face. I rolled over to my side. Ouch. Damn it.

Was someone pinching my nose? I cracked open my eyes. I saw a small beaked face with two beady little black eyes tracking my every motion. My eyes flew all the way open and I rushed more fully awake. I clambered to my feet, nearly rolling over my own limbs. Holy shit! Oh for crap's sake how had a bird gotten - I looked around and I was no longer in my cell. I was out at the campsite that I'd been to so many years ago.

"I don't think we're in Kansas anymore, Toto," I said, glancing at my little birdy friend. When I glanced at it, I had to do a double-take. He had a fat, little, white belly and wings that bled from blue to black. When he launched himself into flight, I realized the middle of his wings were white. His tail gleaned from an iridescent blue to black in the sun. His little beak was black to match the rest of him. He was a funny-looking bird. He dipped and swooped just above my head.

"If you shit, I'm going to roast you over a spit," I called after it. Okay, maybe I wouldn't, but still. This crazy bird was dive bombing me! Just as I thought I was about to be pecked to death, he landed on my shoulder.

"Man, you're a weird little bird. I think we need to find you some little birdy Xanax," I quipped. His pointed gaze was fixed at my feet. I followed his line of sight and sitting at my feet was another damned bird. I bent down and offered the little thing my finger. As I got closer I realized he stood on an envelope. The bird hopped on my finger as though it had no fear of people at all. At the same time, I picked up the envelope.

"Man, I don't know where y'all are coming from, but I'm running out of room," I said as I placed him on my other shoulder. I flipped the envelope or what I assumed to be a letter over. There was a small red wax seal. It was that of the Coven. I flipped it to the front and saw my name scribed in Mil's handwriting. It was the letter. I tore into it in a hurry. Clearly, my flighty friends did not approve of the sudden movement due to their sudden squawking. When I opened the letter, there was an old nursery rhyme written on it. It was about the Magpie. *Oh, that's what these birds are.* The number of them had a meaning. I scanned the nursery rhyme: Two for joy. The two birds leapt into the air and flitted about me. Just before one darted away, he dropped something on my head. Fearing the worst, my hands flew to my hair. I didn't find something wet, but something hard. I pulled it off my head to inspect what the little bird had dropped. It was a small gold coin. One side had a spoked wheel and the other had the face of a bear. The coin melted into my skin, disappearing.

My eyes flew open and I was panting. I raised a hand to my head, but there was nothing there. Then I pulled my hands down to view them. No coin, nothing. *What the crap kind of dream was that?* I pressed my hand to my heart in reflex. My heart was racing as though I'd just run a marathon. I looked over at the small clock at my bedside table. It read 11 p.m. I frowned at the time. Had Mark been by and I just slept through it? No. I tried to brush off the sense of unease I was feeling.

I would say I was getting so sick of these weird-ass dreams, but it was a welcome distraction. I'd not had a single dream like I used to have since I was turned. It weirded me out to think that the strange man who had been present in nearly all of my dreams since I was a child was suddenly gone. Hell, when I woke up from my so-called death, I didn't know if I still had my power. This felt like a dream from him, the strange man. Next time I see him, I'll have to ask for his name.

Delaney, you do realize how insane that sounds right? Great, now I'm talking to myself.

A brisk knock sounded at the door. I heard the clicks and slides for the locks. Then without waiting for a response, Mark rushed into the room. He only carried a wrapped sandwich. He looked wild-eyed and frantic.

"Geez, Mark. What if I'd been naked? And you're late," I chided in a flippant tone. I was trying to lighten the mood he had just dragged about ten feet down. The truth was, he looked uneasy and it was making me worry.

"Listen, I don't have much time. I slipped something in Mitch's food. It was tasteless and odorless. It had some silver in it so he won't heal, just as you didn't. I'll help you as much as I can, but you have to incapacitate him. You can't kill him, neither can I, but you can knock him down for a time and then you'll ..." His words were coming in rapid succession, yet with the last word he trailed off trying to stifle a wince.

"What, Mark?" My words were just as hurried and frantic as his were.

"You're going to have to nearly kill me. Or he won't believe I didn't help you."

I sucked in a breath. Shit, I did not want to hurt him. Not now, anyway. If I'd been asked about a month ago, I would have said I would have used him as a human lightning rod. In that moment, I wasn't so sure I could.

He placed his hands on my shoulders and squeezed them.

"Look, you need to get close to him. Like really close."

His gaze was flickering from brown to green and back again. How close did I need to get?

My eyes narrowed, then widened, "Fuck."

"He's going to be on guard if you come on too strong, but yes, Delaney, you need to catch him with his guard down."

I was going to have to get really cozy with a man whom I despised. And I had to do so without vomiting all over him. *Though now that I think about it, the idea does sound somewhat appealing.* I tried to harden myself to the idea. Somewhere deep down inside myself, I knew that if I did this, a little part of me would die; a piece of my soul would wither and decay and I would never be the same for it. He would make me less of a person and I would allow it, all for the end game. I had to suck it up and swallow down the self-hatred I was feeling.

Mark must have seen the weary look in my eyes because his tone seemed to soften. "I wish I could take back the pain I did not prevent. But, Delaney, I can't." He took in a deep breath and then let it out. "I'll live with the guilt of this for the rest of my life. Mitch could give two shits about the weres as a whole, or even this pack. He is all about power and amassing a ton of it through you."

Just as I was about to ask him what that meant, he stood up and gave me a pointed look. Then he crossed to the door and walked out. I flopped back on the bed. My head was reeling from the knowledge of what I needed to do and my heart was aching for Reid. God, I did not want to do this. Even the new beast that wars inside me agreed that this would be the best way to get out of here and get as far as I could before he came after me. Not a minute later, another knock sounded at the door.

"Sorry, the party was canceled and the hookers have all gone home," I called to the door. I knew who it was. There was only one male who smelled of leather and menace. Mitch. Well, it's now or never. Ready to hate yourself forever? God, when did I become so cynical?

Oh yeah, when I was killed by the bastard I'm about to grind on.

I took a deep breath and sighed, "You don't need me to invite you in, you're not a damn vampire. And even if I did say no, you would …" I trailed off at the

sound of the locks clicking and the door opening. *Gods,*
help me.

DELANEY HAGEN

SiX

I WASN'T SURE what I expected to see when he entered the room, but the look on his face was slightly crazed and crestfallen. What could he be so tortured about? He had beaten me once before and he certainly did not seem to feel anything other than smugness about it. Granted, it was tenfold worse this time. My guard shot up. Could he be feeling bad about what happened? I dismissed that thought as soon as it entered my mind. There was no way. He was incapable of feeling anything other than something that served him.

He walked over to me and knelt at the side of the bed where I sat. He reached up to run a finger along my face. I had to stifle a shudder of disgust. I couldn't help but wince. His hand dropped next to me and he clenched it into a fist and then relaxed. He did this several times before I tore my attention away and looked at him. He was mixed with emotions. I couldn't for the life of me read any of them.

"Delaney, I …" His voice was gruff and he seemed to choke on the words.

"Why are you here, Mitch? Did you come back to finish the job?" I couldn't keep the acid from my words. God, I needed to bury the hate I had for him so I could go find Reid.

Remember, Delaney, the end game. The end game is Reid.

"I regret what I did to you. I just want you and every time you deny me, I lose it."

His words. They sounded like a lie. I didn't believe he wanted me. He just wanted to use me and wanted what I could give him. I didn't believe for one second Mitch's end game was some government shit. I just didn't know what it was.

Older werewolves can sometimes tell when someone is lying. Their ability was not consistent or perfect, but sometimes, if the person was outright lying, they could tell. I was going to have to get rather inventive when it came to these next words.

"Mitch, I forgive you." *For wearing that heinous shirt.*

My tone was solemn. I had to convince him that I did, in fact, forgive him.

His head shot up and his jaw slackened. He was shocked.

Thank God he believed that.

"Mitch, listen. I have had a lot of time to think and I need to try to make the best of this situation." *I'm a changed person.* "I need to make the best of it. So, I'm willing to give you a shot, if you will give me some freedoms."

His eyes widened and his expression went from dumbfounded to elation in the blink of an eye. Then, he grabbed my hand and shot up, pulling me into his arms in one swift motion. I was circled in his arms. I tried to melt into him, but I found myself stiff. I closed my eyes and pictured Reid holding me and I remembered how his warmth would heat my skin to the point of madness. I softened slightly and Mitch seemed to do so as well.

"Delaney, you don't know how long I have waited for you to say this. From the moment I met you, I wanted you. I'll give you as much freedom as I can."

His arms tightened then he released me and he grasped my chin harshly.

"I feel bad about how harsh I was to you. But, Delaney, if you give yourself to me, I'll deny you nothing."

His arm that grasped my hip began to squeeze me tightly, nearing pain.

"Betray me, Delaney, and I'll do far worse to you. And it will kill me to do it."

The look in his eyes was deadly.

Chills ran up my spine. I knew in that moment that if this didn't work he wouldn't kill me, but I would beg him to at every turn. He was being blinded by how badly he wanted me. I had to seize the opportunity. I couldn't give him time to really analyze my words or their meanings.

"Mitch, I know." My voice was weak with fear, but he mistook it for arousal. He pulled me to him. His hard chest was slightly warm against my skin. I felt his shaft grow hard. He pressed me tighter to him, nearly grinding his erection against my pelvis. *Oh, God, I can do this. Don't throw up.*

He leaned down to me and his mouth hovered just above mine.

He whispered huskily, "Meet me, Delaney, and show me you want this."

Now or never. I lifted my face to his more fully and stood on my toes. I brushed my lips with his and started a slow, tentative kiss. He deepened it. I had to open my mouth to invite him in. My stomach tried to lurch, but I clamped down on it. His hands slid from my hair down my back to my ass. I felt my heart dying with every moment I allowed him to kiss and touch me. *Would Reid forgive me? Would he understand?*

Suddenly, his hands grabbed my ass and he lifted me up. Instinctively, I wrapped my legs around his waist and he groaned into my mouth. He pulled away. His eyes were now glowing neon green.

"Delaney, your lips are addictive," he rasped.

"Take me to the bed, Mitch," I nearly choked the words out.

His eyes widened at the request, but his arousal grew. I could scent it. I remembered Reid. I thought of how I felt when he touched me. When he kissed me. I grew slightly aroused, but for Reid. I had to hold on to that for Mitch to believe it was for him. Fooling a human was easy, fooling this being took some major thought.

He let me down and then walked over to the bed and lay on his back. He put his arms under his head and he looked at me as though he were waiting for something.

"Take your clothes off for me," he said in a low, guttural tone. His bulge was straining against his pants.

I faked a smile and slowly pulled my shirt over my head. Then I unclasped my bra. The moment my breasts were free he groaned low in his chest. I slipped my fingers under the hem of my shorts and slowly slid them down my hips. There I stood, in front of the man I hated most in the world, completely bare. I closed my eyes tight. I was trembling with self-hatred.

"Come here, wolf," he said in a near growl.

I opened my eyes and his shirt was off. He was a beautiful man, I could admit that, yet I hated him so much I saw nothing but disgust. *Delaney, you don't have to go all the way, you just need to get close.* I steeled my resolve and walked over to him. I climbed up on the bed and threw my leg over him. My sex rested above his throbbing erection which, thank God, was still inside his pants.

He sucked in a breath. His hands went to my breasts and I shuddered, clenching my teeth and trying to fight the instinct that was screaming at me to fight this. Fight his touch. I moaned, trying to fake as much as I could. He ran his thumb over a nipple, causing the peak to pebble. I ran my hands down his chest. He raised his head to my breast and darted a tongue over one nipple. My nails raked down his chest at the new touch. I tried not to lash out. He then pulled the nipple into his mouth and groaned around it. Shit. This was not helping my arousal; if anything, it was going to kill it. I had to do something and fast. I shifted my leg slightly and angled it so that my knee rested between his legs. *Now or never, Delaney.* I used nearly all of my resolve and rammed my knee into his groin.

His eyes went wide and he shoved me off of him so hard that I went flying backward off the bed. He was heaving breaths in and out and his big hands were covering his crotch. He was writhing in pain. I scrambled to my feet and began to pull lightning from my core. I rushed to him and his eyes were wild and furious.

He snarled at me through clenched teeth, "You fucking bitch! I'll kill you for this."

I didn't waste time with a retort. I went to place my hand directly over his heart, and one of his hands shot out to grab at me, but this motion must have caused him pain because his movements were sluggish. I batted his hand away with no thought. Was that a bone in his arm that I just heard snapping? No, it couldn't be.

Shaking my head, I put a hand over his heart and willed the lightning in my body to leave, pushing everything I had through my hands. The lightning left me with searing pain, but it was nothing to what I knew he was feeling. His body jerked violently in seizure-like movements. His skin around my hand blackened and the room filled with the stench of burning things. Never had I ever put this much power, my power, into something. I didn't want to stop; I wanted to pour everything I had into him until he was nothing but a pile of ash. Because then he would see what he had done to me.

But, I became physically pained. This was the pain I felt when I tried to kill him last time. I pulled away from him knowing my skin was sparking with power. I backed away from his unmoving form lying on the bed. Had he not been weakened by whatever Mark gave him, he would already be healing. I ran to the pile of clothes and found jeans and a long-sleeved shirt. I threw them on. I had no time. I tossed another shirt on over the long-sleeved one. It would be cold, and I didn't have a jacket. I spared one more glance at the nearly charred body lying unmoving on the bed and left the room.

I headed for the stairs, but paused. I ran to Mitch's office. It was locked. I rammed my shoulder, hoping the door would give. It did with surprising ease. I guess I was stronger than I thought. I ran to the desk and pulled out my purse, then ran to the file cabinet and grabbed everything in the C section and stuffed it into my bag. I would have to thank Troy for talking me into buying a bag I could carry a toaster oven in. I ran out of the office and paused at the door to my room, sparing one second to lock all of the locks.

Like that will really do any good.

I hustled down the stairs, frantic, and ran into the room just to the right of the stairs. It was where the other guard typically sat. That's where I found Mark. His eyes met mine and he got out of his chair.

"Don't take any of the cars. He will trace you that way. Take this," he said, handing me a large jug of bleach and a small black phone. My eyes widened. I wasn't planning on doing laundry.

"You need to dunk yourself. Get as far as you can then go to a hotel. Bathe in this and that should get rid of your scent long enough to get away from him."

I nodded.

"Thank you."

He finally met my eyes and they looked pained.

"Wait, where is Reid?"

"I don't know, Mitch never told any of us. I'm betting Dillon knows, but, Delaney, you need to get as far from this place as you can." His words were rushed.

"Okay. What now?" I said in a frustrated tone.

"I'm so sorry, Delaney. I need you to put me out." His tone was full of regret and sadness. He was sorry, or he was a fantastic actor.

I pulled enough lightning to my palm from my core to knock him out for a solid day. This was the last of my power before I would be tapped out. There was a glowing ball of lightning sitting in my hand. He looked down at it and swallowed.

"You ready?" I asked. My voice shook with emotion. I knew he wouldn't die from this, but it still hurt to do this to him.

He nodded. I shoved my hand against his chest. His form went limp and began convulsing on the floor. I gritted my teeth and choked back my tears for him before running to the front door and flinging it open. The cool air was more than welcome to my overheated skin. I'd no freaking idea where I was going, but I had to get there.

I ran. I ran into the night and didn't stop for hours. I was depleted of my lightning, emotionally I was a wreck, and I was only slightly closer to getting to Reid. Somehow the physical strength I was feeling was like nothing I'd ever felt before. The sun was coming, up and I knew I needed to go bleach myself.

I ran to a Walmart and bought some new clothes with what little money I had. With the rest of the money, I found a POS hotel. I needed to sleep, but needed to do this more. I poured the jug into the bath and filled it the rest of the way with water. I got in and dunked myself. My skin burned. I nearly jumped out to rid myself of the foul liquid. I drained the tub and showered off, smelling like a mix between a pool boy and a maid. I tore the tags off my newly purchased clothes and slipped them on. I sighed at the feeling of finally having underwear on.

Walking to the bed, I collapsed on it and tried to figure out what my next move was. I tried to make a decision that Mitch would never expect. I tried to think, but my head was foggy and I was exhausted. I closed my eyes and surrendered to the exhaustion and tumbled head first into the blackness.

REiD JAMiSON

SEVEN

FUCKING TENNESSEE. HE had me in fucking freezing-ass Tennessee. In a state where if someone sees a wolf in their backyard they shoot first and ask questions later. I'd been shot at no less than six goddamned times. It had taken me hours just to reach some kind of civilized town. And then it took about two hours to be able to maneuver myself around enough to get the buckshot that was embedded in my ass out. All in all, I counted myself as lucky, as it could have been worse. It made me wonder. Surely, they would know what I had done by now. I just prayed I knew Mitch. I prayed that I knew him well enough to know he wouldn't kill Delaney.

I was about twenty miles outside of Nashville. I had to find some cash and a way to communicate with Delaney. My thoughts slid back to the god in my dream.

I wonder, if I slept, if I could get him to deliver a message.

Yeah, I could see that conversation.

"Oh, excuse me, oh god who is playing a game with my life, I was wondering if you could deliver a message to someone for me?" Yeah, I really did not think that would fly. This whole time I'd been thinking three and sometimes four steps ahead and it had gotten me nowhere. I needed to take this one step at a time.

Okay, step one: Get some cash for clothes. Then get a phone. I wouldn't let myself look further ahead than that. Now, I needed to figure out a way to get some cash. I did still have that coin. I could pawn it and get some cash. The idea settled in my mind and I pushed on through the gray sleeting rain. While the place where I was kept had a fresh blanket of snow on the ground, the farther south I traveled the more things were melting. The landscape that was once painted in white and shadows morphed into a full gray scale. It looked dirty with the slush and grime.

The near nothingness began to change into a more city-like landscape. I happened upon a pawn shop and I got a little over two thousand dollars for the coin. I did have a thought that I should have kept the coin, but the usefulness had been spent as the spokes on the wheel were gone and the wolf's head had also disappeared for good. It was nearly two ounces of gold and with gold prices high, it was a good deal. They did, however, think I was out of my mind for only having shorts on. I told them I was getting ready for a polar bear dip. Their looks remained horrified. I went to a Walmart and bought clothes and a prepaid phone.

Now, what? I honestly had no idea. It wasn't that I had no idea where she was. I mean not really. Mitch would have kept her in his place in Atlanta. For some reason my inner beast bristled at the thought that she was there. The idea felt wrong. Almost as though I was missing something. Then a crazy idea popped into my head. I could always call Mitch. Okay, the idea was insane, but I could gauge him, see if there was anything I could pick up from the conversation. It was completely unexpected, that's for sure. I knew Mitch well enough to know that it was possible to goad him into saying things he wouldn't normally. I picked up the phone and dialed.

"Hello? Mitch Saldana's phone." The voice was low and smooth.

Who the hell had Mitch's personal cell phone?

"Who is this?" I said in a perplexed tone. Then I heard a groan of pain.

"This is Mark, and you are?" He was clearly annoyed.

"This is Reid. You have my mate." I was snarling, but I couldn't help it. I could just picture Mark's craggy face as I was fighting his alpha.

"Oh, for the gods' sake. Did Delaney get to you already?" His tone went from annoyed to rushed and quiet. He sounded as though he was whispering into the phone. I was taken aback. Then the full force of his words hit me like a train impact.

"Get to me? I only just got out last night. Where the hell is she?" And why would you tell me, I wanted to add, but I didn't want to dissuade him from giving me any information. My heart was pounding so hard I thought it might beat its way through my chest.

"I should have known there was an issue when the guards didn't make their last check-in call," he said in a distracted tone.

"Dammit, Mark, where is she?" I was nearly yelling into the phone, but I didn't care. I glanced around the nearly abandoned park, and there was no one in sight, nor could I scent anyone. This whole conversation wasn't going like I thought it would.

"She got out last night. Listen, I don't have much time. Mitch will be up in a few hours. He hurt her and I wasn't okay with it. I helped her get out. I don't know where she went." I put my hand on the back of the bench and clenched the rough wood. I closed my eyes. Out of that whole statement the words, "He hurt her" hit me like a physical punch to the gut. My vision went red, and my hearing went completely out. He had hurt her, and I wasn't there to protect her. I was only a moment from turning and losing myself to the rage. My muscles distended and I could feel myself slipping both physically and mentally. There was this annoying buzzing noise that I needed to remember. I kept hearing it and trying to remember why it was important.

"Reid, did you hear me?" Mark's voice seemed to bounce me back.

"What?" I snarled, trying to focus on his tone. My own words were garbled.

"Look, there is a ton of the pack here. I can't talk long. I didn't know where you were so I didn't know where to tell Delaney to go. But I gave her bleach to help with the trail. We can't move until Mitch wakes. I slipped him a silver mix to slow his healing and help her get further." His words were coming faster now and growing more panicked.

"Why did you help her?" I questioned. Did he have an underlying motive?

"Because she was kind to me when she had no reason to be, and she took the pain that was meant for me." His voice was pained.

"Mark, thank you. Where do I go? Did she tell you anything?" Now my tone matched his panicked one.

"No. All I can say is she's not in Atlanta. I can't talk though. Mitch will be conscious in a number of hours. I did what I could to help her." I was about to thank him, but I heard the telltale click of an ended call.

I dropped my head and raised my hand to rub the nape of my neck. My head was spinning from all of the information. Had Mark helped Delaney? Why? Had he lied? His words sounded true, but after having been fooled by Mitch in the past, I had little trust left for anyone. I'd no idea where she would go. My heart leaped. She had gotten herself to safety. My chest swelled with pride at the knowledge that my female was strong. Like another blow, Mark's words reverberated through my mind. He had hurt her. Hurt her so much that Mark feared for her and felt the need to step in. The rage in me swelled and nearly spilled over. I would kill him. But, when I did, I would do it so it would be slow and oh so painful. The beast stirred.

Shit, my thoughts were everywhere. I needed to focus on Delaney and how to know where she was. She had no family. Not anymore. I heard a strange squeaking tweeting noise. I peered around and my eyes settled on a pair of strangely marked birds. They were a deep blue, nearing on black with white markings on their wings. They were small birds.

Unlike a chickadee or sparrow, these birds had this half-squawk, half-tweet thing going on. The birds were making enough noise that they could set off a car alarm. The pair sat perched about twenty feet away, behind the bench I was sitting on. I couldn't concentrate with these crazy birds fighting over a scrap of bagel. And yet, the infuriating birds grew louder. Did they have a death wish? I got up and stormed over to the pair. As soon as I neared, they flew off, leaving behind their query. Just before I walked off to contemplate where Delaney could have gone, the item the birds were fighting over caught my eye. It wasn't food at all. It was, in fact, a scrap of paper. I bent down to pick it up and scanned the paper. It looked to be a scrap of a travel magazine or National Geographic. On one side there was part of what looked like an article about Ancient Greece or maybe Rome. I scanned the paper further. I flipped the scrap and saw a picture of a coastline. There were no markers to identify where this coast was. I flipped back to the article. I tried to read the small section I could see..

"This section of land once thought to be … Though both works suggest that the ancient city lay on the coast … Most

historians agree that the Great War could have been in the twelfth, thirteenth, or fourteenth centuries BCE."

The paper was torn and cut off on the edges making the information sparse and broken.

"Though some historians and archaeologists agree that the site of the great city and the war itself are merely a legend, there is evidence ... Trojan."

I shook my head at the paper and balled it up. I almost felt silly for getting so distracted by two birds and a scrap of a magazine. I tried to focus again on the problem at hand. Where would she go? No family, no friends. She wouldn't go to her apartment. That sucker was long gone. She would never go back to Mil's. Would she even go back to Savannah? I let out a long breath. I had no idea, and it was infuriating!

Just as I went to toss the ball of paper in my hand, I paused. I opened it again and smoothed the wrinkles out on my knee. The article spoke of a city and a war. Trojan. It was clearly the city of Troy. My eyes widened. I folded the paper and shoved it in my pocket. I nearly leaped off the bench.

I tilted my face to the sky and said, "Tricky god."

Before heading south, I picked up the phone and dialed one more number. I prayed I remembered it correctly.

"Hello?" I nearly sighed at the slightly Creole voice.

"Oh, thank God. Monique? It's Reid."

"Oh, my gracious. Reid, I just spoke with Delaney. Michael, I mean Mitch, has her." Her tone neared distraught.

"She got away. But, listen. Are you up for a trip? I think we are going to need your help."

She let out a deep breath. "This will be a betrayal to the Coven."

"Monique, please." I was not above begging her.

"I didn't say no. The inner circle has lost their minds. Bernard has become increasingly mad. They have been forcibly breeding the witches on the reservation for the past three years. And …" Her voice cracked with emotion. "… Gods, things here are bad. They are gearing up for something, and they have to be stopped. Agree to help me with the Coven, and I'll come to help you."

I groaned at the thought of yet more to do, but if we were going to protect Delaney and stop Mitch, we needed all the help we could get.

"Agreed. Listen, I have a pretty good idea where she's headed, and I want you to get there as fast as possible." I gave her the address, hoping I recalled it correctly. I needed to trust my instincts on this, and they were screaming that this was where Delaney would be going.

"I'm officially renouncing any connection with the Coven. I'll help stop Mitch and, Reid …" Her tone turned serious, and it held a biting edge to it as she spoke her last words, "... I'll kill him."

"Yeah, well, get in line," I quipped.

We said our goodbyes and I hung up the phone and shoved it into my pocket. My ID card was long gone, so a plane ticket was out of the question. I would run there if I had to. I knew what I had to do. No matter how I got there, I had to get to her. My resolve steeled. I would get to her. I began walking south. With every step, I was one step closer to her. Closer to having my heart back.

MiTCH SALDANA
EiGHT

PAIN RADIATED THROUGH my whole body. I was a fucking alpha and should be healing after what that little cunt did to me. Yet, there I was, conscious, but my body wouldn't allow me to wake. I could feel my nerves firing and my muscles contracting and relaxing as I was healing from the inside out. It struck me as odd as fuck that the process was taking this long. I was close to being able to talk. I could feel my skin beginning to heal now. Hours I lay there. Hours after that bitch did this to me. I tried to move a hand to my balls, which were still aching, both from being so turned on and from her knee connecting

1

with them. My hand twitched. That small motion meant that I would be up and moving very soon.

My healing seemed to be slowed. But how? I tried to trudge through my fogged memories to what could have caused this. I had this niggling thought that I was trying desperately to ignore. It wouldn't go away though. Then I pushed the thought to the fore. It had to be one of my own helping the witch. Who longed for death as much as to have done this?

"Alpha, would you join me for coffee?" Mark's words played over again in my head. While at the time I saw nothing in them, now, as I played the conversation back, his actions did seem odd. He was nervous. The muscle near his right eye ticked. No, not Mark. I again tried to push the memory aside. He would never betray me. Now I was able to move my fingers at will.

Again my thoughts slid to Mark. After I called him to take a passed-out and beaten Delaney to her room, the look on his face, what was it? He was horrified. At the time, I thought he was afraid that I would do the same to him. Maybe it wasn't fear. Had he let her out and she was protecting him? No. Why would she?

Again, I dismissed the memories. I could now lift both hands from the bed. My skin felt tight over my chest as it healed. To say the process was painful would be a vast understatement.

Mark found me at some point, but I had no recollection of time. I was unconscious for quite a while. I was boiling with rage and as soon as I could get up from this fucking bed, I would lay waste to anyone and everyone that little bitch cared for. Reid was as good as dead. That thought alone helped speed up the healing. My eyes were open. I could move my head back and forth and even move my feet around. To pass the time, I thought of my goal. I told everyone this whole thing was about taking over the supernatural world and then the world of the humans. Really it was far more simple. It was about amassing power. My goal was about being the most powerful being and then slowly killing off anyone who stood in my way. And if that fucking meant killing a god, I would do it. I did want to rule the world, but not for the werewolves. I wanted to be the one with the power. I knew I couldn't do this without Delaney. I thought I could possess her by threatening her, beating her or even seducing her. Now, it has become painfully clear that she would never bend to me. Now there was only one thing I could do.

I would need to kill Reid and then use her to take out the Coven. But as soon as I did that, I would have to kill her. And if it came down to it, I would kill her before taking out the Coven. While the prophecy stated that she would bring them down, I still had an ace up my sleeve. Something I'd told no one. I lifted my head off the bed and struggled to sit. After six attempts, I sat up fully. I was nearly healed. I reached for my cell phone to call the pack, but I could feel they were mostly already here. There were noises bellowing from below. Good, at least someone was doing their fucking job. I was so often the only one who did anything around here, it was refreshing that someone else did something right.

Distantly I heard my cell phone ring, but clearly some thoughtful, yet misguided person took it out to let me heal. I pulled myself to my feet and made my way on unsteady feet to the door. I smelled of burnt feathers and charred plastic. I cared little. I had to find Delaney. Surely she was stopped by Mark, who had downstairs duty. Either that or she incapacitated him. I slowly made my way down the mountain of stairs. I could finally give the order to kill that piece of shit Reid. Maybe I wouldn't. Maybe I would go there and do it myself. My mouth watered and my cock stiffened at the thought of it.

At the bottom of the stairs, just off to the left, I heard the rumble of several members of the pack. But I veered right to the sound of one muffled voice. I'd no idea why my instinct told me to go this way, but I had learned to trust it. I felt a chill run up my back. I heard a lone voice coming from just ahead of me. Clearly the person was trying to be quiet. I didn't know why this seemed odd to me, but my hackles were most definitely raised. I strained to hear the person's voice.

"Mitch will be up in a few hours. He hurt her and I wasn't okay with it. I helped her get out. I don't know where she went." I knew the voice, and the betrayal stung. The hurt was overshadowed by pure rage. I'd hurt Delaney, and the thought of what I'd done to her turned me on. I pushed the memories out and tried to focus on Mark's voice.

"Because she was kind to me when she had no reason to be, and she took the pain that was meant for me." His tone held a note of pain. Pain that was meant for him? I knew she couldn't have gotten out by herself. I would kill him for this. My vision was wavering from clear to fogged by the red of rage. There was a pause in the conversation. Then a thought hit me, who could he be talking to? Could more of my pack be against me than I thought? I needed to let this play out, so even though it went against everything my beast was screaming, I did not interrupt the conversation.

In a tone so low I had to strain to hear, Mark said, "No. All I can say is she's not in Atlanta. I can't talk though. Mitch will be conscious in a number of hours. I did what I could to help her." I assumed he hung up because I didn't hear anything else. I waited a few heartbeats and walked into the room.

"Mark." I had to fight to make my voice even. It came out forced the best I could manage considering I was nearly choking on rage.

He jumped at the sound of my voice. It was obvious I rattled him. Good. He looked at me and his eyes went wide. The beast inside me riled at the sight of his discomfort.

"You seem surprised to see me," I quipped.

"Oh, no I'm sorry, I was just startled," he replied calmly. While the words were true, his calm was feigned.

"Fill me in. I don't recall what happened after that bitch put me out," I spat the words. I was pissed and I was only a hair away from losing it completely. But I needed to get as much information from him as I could. I did not want him to think I heard him.

"My memory is a bit fuzzy as well. I heard some thuds and moans and thought she had given herself to you, so I settled down. I must have dozed off because the next thing I heard were footsteps coming down the stairs. I thought it was you until I scented her, but she rushed me and sent a jolt through me. I nearly pissed myself. I woke up and she was gone. When I went to check on you, you were badly burned and not healing well, so I set in the protocol. I gathered the pack and sent a small group to track her down. I haven't heard from them yet." His tone was even. Too even, as though he was forcing it.

"Also, um, sir. I have not heard from either of the guards." Now, these words he was stuttering over.

"What? Have you accessed the security footage?" I was almost afraid to ask. Then the scent in the air changed. It became metallic and sweet. I breathed it in deeply. Fear. I shuddered at the tantalizing scent. My eyes slid shut for a brief moment. Mark must have been convinced that I hadn't heard him because this was the first time since I entered the room that he exhibited this amount of fear. I blinked and peered over at him. I knew my eyes had begun to glow at his uneasy expression.

"Um, well, no I'd not gotten there yet. But, I'll do it now." He nearly tripped over the words. I waited, unmoving. I didn't dare look at the screen. I had a sinking feeling I knew who he was on the phone with and it only enraged me more. He turned and the look on his face was confirmation enough.

I turned to the wall at my back and punched a hole in it. There was no pain, there was only the pleasure of destruction. *Everything is falling apart.* I needed to kill something. I was unraveling and I was losing control. I'd suspected that Reid was gone after the conversation

I overheard, but hadn't wanted to believe it. My vision was hazing and I knew the beast was throwing itself at the sides of its cage.

I felt arms pulling on my shoulders. The touch seemed to help clear my vision slightly. I realized that I felt soft flesh beneath my now curling claws. I blinked rapidly to aid my vision and felt throbbing under my fingertips. Then the sharp scent of blood assaulted my senses. I thrummed with excitement. Finally, I was able to see that I held Mark up against the wall. My claw-tipped hand was wrapped around his throat. Then my hearing kicked in.

"Mitch, Mitch, can you hear me? You need to let Mark down. We will figure this out."

It was Dillon. I needed? I roared in frustration and incredulity. *The fuck he is going to tell me I need to do anything.* My bellow silenced him and caused Mark to thrash out. *Good, I like the struggle.* My grip was slipping and I was loving every moment of it.

"Need? Oh, you insignificant wolf. I have only one need right now. Mark has betrayed us. Betrayed me. Take him, before I slaughter him." My voice was guttural and dripping with hatred. I stepped back, letting Mark fall to the floor. Dillon tried to go to him and help him up, but Mark waved him away. I didn't know why, but I saw that action as admirable. He stood up, squared his shoulders and narrowed his gaze to me. I nearly lost it again as this was a blatant challenge and the beast in me wouldn't have it.

I swallowed back my disdain to choke out one word, "Why?" It was a snarl, but it was the best I could manage.

"Because you beat her, you abused her in more ways than one, and, above all else, because she didn't deserve it. This prophecy may be true, but nowhere are you mentioned in it, Mitch. You have no right."

I launched myself at him. I laid into him and no one dared stop me this time. I felt my claws sink into flesh. The way the skin tensed under my claws then gave way with a silent pop nearly sent me into a frenzy. I stopped myself, knowing I didn't want to kill him, not yet. I had a plan. I always had a plan. I backed away from Mark's limp, crumpled form lying on the ground. I'd ravaged his neck. His throat was nothing but a mangled mess. Blood dripped from my fingertips to add to the carnage at my feet.

"Take him to the basement." The words were garbled and rough. I wouldn't need to repeat myself though. I absent-mindedly stepped aside, letting Dillon drag Mark away; all the while I was licking my fingers clean. The tangy taste sizzled on my tongue.

"Is it true? Mark let her go?" It was Matthew, my first.

I whirled to face him. Matthew was a big son of a bitch. While he was as tall as me, he was massive, a mixed martial artist before I changed him. He was so tanned, he neared red. The only hair on his head was located along his jaw. It was a black sprinkle, causing him to look harsh. Matthew owned a gym and that made easy pickings for the pack.

"Yes," I said between gritted teeth. My heart was beating so wildly it felt as though my whole body was throbbing.

"Mitch, Reid is gone, or I'm assuming, based on the fact that we haven't heard from the guards. And Delaney is gone. What do we do now?" His voice was even and showed no inflection of fear. He trusted his alpha.

I glanced at him and smiled with all teeth.

"We can't bring down the witches without Delaney. So we need to get her back. I'm betting she went north to save Reid. So we go north." Matthew smiled at the prospect of hunting prey. It's what we lived for. He turned to leave.

"Matthew, do me a favor while I get ready for Mark's …" I trailed off shivering at the thought, "…upcoming treatment."

Matthew eyed me warily, but I could tell by the sour edge to his scent that he was excited. "Yes, alpha?"

"Call Mark's wife. Let her know she is about to be a widow. Also, send Tyler south just in case she was dumb enough to go to Savannah." I waved him away, but not before I saw a smile break out over his cold face.

I walked to my room to ready for Mark and after, we would go north. My instincts were screaming that's where she would run and I needed to trust them. I had a plan I knew would work. I just had to find my little white wolf.

DELANDEY HAGEN

NiNE

SOUTH. THAT'S WHERE I planned to run. Okay, the word plan was a little strong. I had nowhere else to run. So, I ran to the only place where I could gather myself enough to formulate a real plan. *Good lord, I have no idea what I'm doing. This "plan" is so dumb. Maybe Mitch won't think I would be this dumb, so he wouldn't think to look here.*

Seriously, Delaney? Ugh.

I would run to Troy. Okay, so I did realize that he may not be the most stable person I could go to, but he was the only person I had left.

Yeah well, what if you get him killed too? Shut up, self! Ugh. I was losing my mind! I had just enough money to get to Savannah on a bus. This fact, under normal circumstances, wouldn't have been an issue, but now that I had super senses, it was the fifth circle of hell. No, really, I thought it was located under the definition of cruel and most certainly unusual punishment. I nearly trampled every other poor person on that bus of disgust to get out. Now, I needed to walk to Troy's.

Then I had a thought that caused me to pause and ice to wash over me. *What if Mitch has already done something to Troy?* What if … oh God … No, I wouldn't think like that. I did pick up my step, just in case.

IT TOOK ME nearly two hours to walk to Troy's, but I had a weird feeling as I stood outside. I could feel something inside I'd never felt before: a sting of energy. There was a witch inside his house. *Is he in trouble? Okay, calm down, Delaney, rushing in guns drawn won't help.* I took a deep breath and walked to the door. Troy's house was in need of a little of renovation, but it was on the edge of downtown and a great price. Okay, renovation may be too light of a word. The damn place looked as if a strong breeze would bring it crumbling to the ground. Troy called it charming. I called it a fire hazard. The only thing that wasn't kindling was the swing that hung just to the right of the door way.

Just as I went to knock on the door, I heard what sounded like two screaming teenage girls inside. Then, I heard a fire alarm going off. The front door flew open and smoke seemed to create a halo around the form standing in front of me. This form was not Troy. Nor was the power I felt coming from him. His face looked just as shocked as mine. He was about six foot tall and, oh holy hot sauce, he was attractive. He had on a black button-down shirt that was tucked into dark-wash jeans. His hair was a mix of milk and bittersweet chocolate and his eyes nearly matched the shade of his hair. The lines of his face weren't chiseled; it seemed more like they were molded to perfection. His skin was a mix of cream and peach. He was jaw dropping. Literally, if my mouth gaped any larger, a bird might take it as an invitation to build a nest.

Our eyes met and his went wide. Though this man didn't set off any alarm bells, I did not want to take any chances. I pulled lightning from my core to my palms. The feeling of pulling so rapidly, rather than the slow build, burned slightly. His gaze flicked to my sparking hands and his hand flew to his mouth.

He raised his hands up as if to say, "I'm unarmed and I come in peace." All while never taking his eyes off me. Then turned his head and yelled, "Troy, I need you to come to the door." Part of me relaxed at hearing Troy's name. The man's voice held a thick southern accent, but it wasn't anything from Georgia. Texas maybe? His tone, though, was so low that if I had balls, they would surely have been tingling.

"Okay, I'll be there in a second. I'm trying to make sure the house doesn't burn down. Oh Lord, shit!" Troy's voice rang over the sound of spraying. His voice very nearly shattered my fragile heart. I pulled my lightning back to my core.

"Hi, I'm Delaney. I um …"

"Oh, sweet mamajama. Okay, I think I got it out," Troy said, rounding the corner.

Then I saw his face. His perfect face. My heart burst at seeing him. My eyes blurred with unshed tears. His face looked as shocked as I felt. He didn't hesitate, he ran at me. He wrapped me in his arms and I inhaled the scent of him. Clean man and smoke? That was new. I couldn't think, I could only feel. I felt him shudder against me. His whole body was thrumming and I was bawling uncontrollably. He pulled back and looked at me. That's when I saw his face streaked with tears. Belatedly, I realized he was speaking.

"Jesus. I didn't know where you were," he said between sobs.

I began to calm slightly and that's when I realized that the thrumming I felt was power. His body was calling to mine as though he were a ... No. This was the pull I felt when I saw another witch. But that was impossible. Troy wasn't a witch. I placed a hand on his chest and then I felt it, I felt his pull. My eyes widened.

"What. The. Actual. Fuck," I said, as he pulled me past the poor man still standing in the doorway. I heard the door shut with a soft click. The small house smelled of smoke and burnt things. It smelled like most of the homes I ever lived in after I got done with them. God, just being close to Troy like this made me feel more normal, more like me before I became so damaged. Troy pulled me through the foggy house to the kitchen. He whirled to face me and his expression looked bleak. Oh God, my heart broke all over again at that look. He gazed at me as though he was trying to speak, but he couldn't find adequate words to express just what he was feeling.

He took in a deep breath; his expression changed to anger and he erupted, "Where the hell have you been? My life has been falling apart and my best friend was gone. For fucking months! I thought you were dead!"

His words were a knife to my heart.

I felt warm tears stream down my cheeks. I tried to speak, but no words came out. I should have been there for him.

"Shit. I'm sorry. I have gone through hell and back, and I thought you moved again and didn't tell me." In a swift movement, we both sat on the floor right where we stood. He reached out in a motion he's done a thousand times before, but I flinched. He pulled back, but gave me a soft smile. He reached for me again. He cradled my face with both hands and said in a low tone, "Tell me everything."

And I did. I told him every sordid detail, except for the specifics of my torture, not because I wanted to, because I couldn't seem to stop myself. But, damn it, as I spoke my heartfelt lighter. With my words, Troy's face grew more and more incensed. After I finished, he looked much like I felt.

"Troy, I'm sorry I couldn't be here. I wanted to be. Even now, I worry that I have brought you more trouble than even we can handle."

He shook his head in negation. "Fuck that. Let him come at me. I'll burn his ass," Troy said, steeling his face.

"Yeah, so, speaking of that. Got something you want to tell me?" I leaned in close and lowered my tone appreciably, "And this story better include tall, tan and fuckable."

"Lord, woman. Well, that's Garrett. He's, well, my husband."

My eyes nearly bugged out of my skull. *I'm sorry, married?* I whipped my head around searching for the handsome Garrett. He leaned against the doorframe leading from the kitchen to the hallway. He looked not at me, but Troy. He looked at him with longing, as though even this separation was too much. My stomach did a little flip-flop for Troy. I was happy for him.

I opened my mouth to scold him for getting hitched without me, but he held up a hand to silence me. *As if that would stop me. Silly queen.*

"You got married without me!" Then fire erupted from his outstretched hand and just narrowly missed my face. The small blast of fire smacked the wall just behind me with a crack.

"Oh, don't worry, I got it." Garrett's smooth southern voice rang out as he walked over to the smoldering wall. He patted the small mark with his large hand, then gave me a thumbs up.

Stupidly, I raised a shaky hand and returned the gesture. I turned to look at Troy fully. In my best Cuban accent I said, "Lucy, you got some splainin' to do."

"Girl. I don't even know where to start," Troy said, eyeing his hand. He looked at the limb as though it were an unpredictable weapon. He gingerly lowered it to his lap then, clearly thinking better about it, he slipped the hand under his ass to sit on it.

"When did this start? I mean, I have never felt power in you." He looked offended at the admission. So I added, "Troy, I don't mean it like that. I mean I have never felt power in you calling to me the way another witch's power does."

"I think I started feeling weird after I got home from your aunt's requiem."

My eyes widened. No. No. Not possible.

His eyes narrowed at me. "Hooker, you better speak up, because I'm about a cunt hair shy of being a flaming queen. Do you realize just how cliché that is?"

I smiled, I couldn't help it. He was ridiculous, and I loved him for it. Maybe I could make him a shirt that said "Flaming queen." I had to bite my lip to stop from grinning at the thought.

I released the breath I hadn't realized I was holding and explained, "Well, my aunt said that in death a witch can gift her power to someone. She said these were just stories and she had never known anyone it had happened to. But, it would explain this. However, it takes a really powerful witch, like nearing the power of a god. The only way I could see this as a possibility would be a god came down and offered her part of his power. I don't know any gods out there who care that much about me. I mean latent powers are possible, but I would have felt something before."

His eyes bugged. *Oh, lord, he is about to flip.*

"Whoa, wait a second before you flip out. Mil only told me stories about this happening. They were more like myths or tall tales. And did you miss the part about the god?" Out of the corner of my eye, I saw Garrett cross to Troy and settle down behind him. He pulled Troy to his chest and held him there. Troy seemed to melt into the bigger man. I gave Garrett a shy smile. He calmed Troy. And at that moment I knew they were right. He was Troy's missing piece. As much as I loved seeing him happy, it caused a pang in my heart.

Troy's eyes narrowed, "Like werewolves?"

Yeah, well there was that.

"Wait, Mil was an Earth Witch. She couldn't have done this," Troy said in a hopeful tone. He was waiting for me to confirm his words.

Aw shit.

"Well, um not necessary. In the stories she told me, mind you this only happened twice before, the power changed and evolved. You don't know much about witches, you never had the need to know, but our power base comes from our core. Think of it like a well. If you dig and expand your well, it can grow. Now, a witch can grow more powerful, but they do have a cap, a level where their power is at a max. This is different for each witch. I have no idea what determines a witch's power, but I do know it's about the soul and how the soul reacts to that well. It's about how the power settles in you and you have a lot to do with it."

Shit. I was starting to believe this. He had a confused look plastered across his face, so I tried to clarify.

"Look, say Mil had sent me that power. Because of who I am, how the power settles in my core, and simply how the power reacts to me, it might be something entirely different. Power is fickle like that."

"She must have hated me to do this." His tone was resigned. This time I saw it in his face.

"No, she would only gift you with this because she loved and trusted you with it. Our power isn't just an outfit we wear, then discard. It's an integral part of us and part of our spirit. She gave you part of her heart, part of her soul. She will never be complete without it," I said, trying not to cry. I needed one of the pins in my soul to ease.

"I miss the old bat. But, why? Why would she give this to me? All I have done with it is nearly burn everything to the ground …" He trailed off as though his words reminded him of something. "This is how you feel isn't it?"

"Yeah. Like I have way too much power and like this whole thing is a mistake." I realized that it was true. It was how I felt. I felt like I was given all of this power for nothing. I was given this, and it was a mistake because surely a better person would have done more. Maybe, someone less weak could do more. And I wasn't worthy of the gift given to me at birth. I took in a deep breath and released it.

"As to why? Well, I don't know. I think she made the right choice though. If we can get it under control, do you think you'll be okay with it?"

He paused to think about the question. And I realized I'd stopped breathing. His answer mattered to me. It mattered a whole damn lot.

"Well, we will have to get a better teacher than you. No offense, but, D, you do fry more things than a KFC. Except the time you kicked that wolf's ass. But, yeah I'll be okay. I like you witchy type people."

I mocked offense.

"I'll have you know I have much more control over that now," I chided, pointing at him. A small spark fell from my outstretched finger. Oops.

He looked from it and then to me, raising an eyebrow.

"Shut up."

We sat on the hardwood floor. The three of us saying nothing, yet it was so cathartic. With every passing heartbeat, the room seemed to clear, and I grew lighter.

"I have a question," Troy said, breathing the silence.

"Uh oh," Garrett intoned.

Troy elbowed him, causing him to groan.

"Uff, what? Can you blame me? I smell trouble, love."

"Hush you. Um, will you shift? I mean I don't know? Is that rude?"

My eyes widened at him. But, not at the question.

"Since when have you cared if something you said was rude?" I asked, smiling at him. It felt good to smile with him. I stood up. "I'll change for you, I'll need to eat though. I don't have one hundred percent control of everything just yet, so when I change, do me a favor and get something out for me to eat." I left the kitchen and walked into the hallway.

"Eat? Lord. Like what? Cake?" Troy called after me.

I raised an eyebrow at him as if to say, "Really?"

"I'm a wolf, Troy. Meat." I slipped into the small half bath that was tucked into the hall and stripped with quick efficiency. Then, I shifted. My shift held some pain. However, it felt, well, right. Like I'd been missing a part of me this whole time and now I was who I should be. My senses spiked. My beast riled a little at the new hunger pangs, and the dull beating of the heartbeats in the room filled my ears.

I nudged the door of the bathroom open with my nose and loped into the kitchen. Troy stood in the middle of the small room. His jaw was nearly resting on the floor. My eyes flicked to the fluttering pulse at his neck. My mouth watered. I padded over to him. I was not as big as Reid or Mitch. I only stood about four-and-a-half feet tall, whereas both of them were about five foot. I sat in front of him, waiting for him to do something.

He reached a tentative hand out, but before he made contact he withdrew.

"Can I touch you?" His voice wavered.

I ducked my head and snuffled at his hand. He lifted his arm, and I placed my head just under his wiggling fingers.

"Delaney, you're a beautiful woman. I mean, I think I have a better figure …" I eyed him. At my expression, he continued, "But, you're magnificent. You're snow white, and your eyes glow silver. And your fur is soft, but it sparks with static electricity."

"Whoa. Delaney? That you?" Garrett held a plate of something that smelled divine.

I walked over to him. He took a few steps back, and his scent hit me like a ton of bricks. His fear. I growled low in my chest. I knew in my muddled mind that he wasn't prey, but hell he smelled so damned good. I opened my mouth, panting.

27

"Garrett, I think she smells your fear. Put the plate on the floor and back away, okay, honey?" Troy's tone was low and even.

Garrett did as he was instructed. My eyes locked on the plate. I sniffed the air then walked over. Ground turkey? Really? I cocked my head at Troy.

He threw his hands up in exasperation, "Look, I was trying to lose weight. I have to watch my figure. It's all we got. Oh, should we cook ..."

I fell on the food. His words were lost to the sounds of my eating. Though I would have not turned down more, I was sated. I wanted to change back, and now that I gained a little energy, I thought I could. I'd never tried so many fast changes so close together. Changing forms may be easier for me physically, but it took a lot out of me in other ways, like my control and energy. I paused and pulled my human form to the front. Changing my form was about letting the beast form slip past my human form and vice-versa. But, with that comes a game of who controls whom. It's not like there is another being in my body, but another facet of myself. I took a deep breath, and as I slowly released it, my human form eased to the front and I shifted.

I staggered a bit, though I did manage to stay on my feet. I felt Garrett's arm grasp my shoulder helping me. I hadn't realized I was swaying. His warm hand helped to ground me slightly. I turned to him and gave him a soft smile in thanks. Changing forms so fast and close together made my nerves a little raw. I glanced up to find Troy staring at me slack jawed.

"You know, if someone had asked me six months ago if I would have my husband feeling up a naked white girl in my kitchen, I would have thought you were crazy. Yet, here we are."

I looked down and realized I'd forgotten to change in the other room. *Shit.* I covered myself with my arms.

"A little late for modesty, don't you think?"

"Troy, grab my clothes, would you?" I said a little hoarsely.

He tossed a small hand towel at me as he walked to the bathroom. I caught it and said, "This towel ain't gonna cut it."

I heard Troy's voice echo off the walls as he called, "Maybe you should switch to turkey on a regular basis. Then, that towel might work."

He rounded a corner and I tossed the towel in his face.

"Whore," I said, smiling at him.

He chucked my clothes at me and added, "Hooker."

God, how I missed him.

TROY AND HIS new husband, as weird as that was to say, put me in the guest room, which was decorated like something straight out of Moulin Rouge. I knew this would only be a short stay. I couldn't risk bringing Mitch and his pack down on my friends. I needed to find Reid. I had no idea what I was doing.

I flopped my head back on the fluffy pillow. I had the rest of the night and some of tomorrow to decide what I should do. In the meantime, I thought training Troy might do two things: act as a distraction and offer copious amounts of entertainment. But first, I would just close my eyes for a moment. I fell into darkness.

There were two ways people woke up: with lots of yawning and stretching or like their ass was on fire. For some of us, our asses really were on fire. My eyes snapped open and I was assailed by the scent of burning feathers. *Great, glad to know some things didn't change*. I got out of bed and ran to the attached bathroom. I showered and got ready for the rest of the day. When I got back into the room, I couldn't make myself leave. I flopped on the bed, closed my eyes and thought of everything. *Well, that's depressing*. I needed to think about nice things. Like kittens and puppies. It's sad that even my thoughts were jaded. I was actively trying to avoid the one thought that would hurt the most. Reid.

I had no idea how long I laid there. Troy called a few times, but that may have been a dream.

Finally, I peeled myself off the bed that was surely sent down from heaven and made my way downstairs to find Troy.

I found Troy and Garrett on the front porch, sitting on the hanging swing. I was so happy for Troy. He seemed genuinely content. He looked at Garrett the same way I felt about Reid. I felt a pang of sadness. I tried to swallow it back. I tried to tell myself that I would find him, but "myself" was stubborn.

I turned to go back into the house to leave the two alone when I heard Garrett say, "Delaney, hey darlin', do you mind keeping Troy company? I need to get ready for work." He had one of those voices that made a girl want to sigh and fan herself. I nodded as he got up and kissed Troy on the lips. I scooted past him and sat down. We sat in silence for a few moments.

The weather had cooled substantially since the last time I was here. The sun was setting and lent a pink glow to the oak trees and Spanish moss. Savannah, this time of year, was magnificent. The city never turned colors with the changing of the leaves, but rather the changing of the day. The summer nights were oranges and yellows, but the fall and winter it changed to pink and purple. Had I really been in that room for a full twenty-four hours? My stomach gave a growl. Guess so.

"Would you bang him?" Troy asked about the skinny man walking along the sidewalk.

"No way, too skinny. I would break him," I replied. This was our favorite game. Troy, Sierra, and I would sit on this very swing, drinking and playing our bang or no bang game. My heart hurt at the thought that I could never have those times back. The times when I had worries, but they were so distant that they seemed like nothing more than a faint dream. I longed for that time.

"How did you meet Garrett?" I asked, eyeing the empty street.

"He's a firefighter," he replied, with a smile in his voice. Clearly, he was remembering a fond time. *A time I should have been here for.*

"I might be able to help you control it, you know? I mean, I can try anyway." I looked at him more fully. His eyes sparked with hope.

"Well, this is my new normal, so let's get this party started." He eyed me, waiting for instruction.

"First, close your eyes."

He raised an eyebrow, but did as I instructed.

"This may sound strange, but turn your gaze inward and look for your core. Try to find that place where you feel your power the strongest."

He squinted in concentration. Then his eyes flew open.

"Holy shit, I feel it." He sounded so shocked.

I smiled. I placed my hands on my lap, palms up. I pulled my lightning out. It formed two small balls of sparking electricity. Troy's eyes bugged at the sight. I don't think I'd ever done this with him. This moment reminded me of Sierra, and I felt so much emotion it nearly hurt. I pushed the thoughts aside and tried to focus on helping Troy.

"Okay, you need to pull a thread from it. Imagine you're taking a small pinch. If you grab too much power, you may not be able to control it. So, pull a small pinch. Pull it through your core up your chest, down your arms, and have it settle in your hands. Most witches have their power form a ball or other small object. Mil told me that fire witches were a lot like me in that their power is harder to manipulate. I do know fire witches can form a ball or even a flame." A confused look flashed across his face. "Sorry, I know it's a lot. Okay, I would go with a ball shape. Try it. Pull it slowly."

I pulled the small orbs of lightning back into my core. It caused a tingle to run up my spine. Troy's eyes slid shut and he flipped his palms up on his lap. After about two minutes of trying, I began to see a flicker form in his right hand. It grew to about the size of a gumball. It looked like a tiny sun hovering in his hand.

"Troy, open your eyes," I said in a low tone. He slowly cracked his eyes and peered down at his hand.

"Holy shit! I did it!" he exclaimed. The small orb flew out of his hand out into the front yard. The small flame began to smolder slightly. Our gazes met, and we both ran to the small flame that had grown slightly in the dry grass. We both began stomping on the smoking ground, trying to put the embers out. After a few moments of panic, the disaster was averted. *This might not be as easy as I thought.* We couldn't help but laugh. Hey, at least we didn't cause a forest fire; Smokey would be so proud.

"I don't think I'll be getting my security deposit back," Troy said, peering down at the dinner plate-sized burnt hole in the ground. We both walked back to the porch when I had an idea.

"Hey, do you have a lighter?" I asked, quirking my head at him.

"Yeah in the kitchen. To the right of the stove."

I ran into the house. I rounded the corner and ran smack into Garrett. I bounced off him and went sprawling on my ass. Yup, still the same old me. I shook my head and stood up. Man, I have the grace God gave a three-legged dancing hippopotamus.

"Ouch, you shocked me," he said, hand going to his chest.

Shit.

"Sorry, I didn't see you there," I said, walking to the drawer. I found the small red lighter and turned to leave.

"Listen," Garrett said, rubbing the nape of his neck. "Please do me a favor. I love that boy out there. He puts on a happy face, but I know he's been through a lot in the past few months, so if you're only going to bring him more pain ... Well, I'll have to ask you to leave." His words found their way directly to my heart and nearly sliced it into small unrecognizable pieces. This man loved Troy. I did too. I knew he was right. I did not want to cause my friend any more pain than I already had.

I smiled and said softly, "I'm glad Troy has you."

We both walked out of the house. Garrett gave Troy a swift kiss and then walked to his car and pulled away.

I motioned for Troy to stand with his back to the door of the house. I stood in front of him and held up the lighter.

"Okay, let's try this," I said as I raised my hand up between us, palm up. I flicked the lighter over my palm. The spark flew from the lighter and I pulled it to my hand. The flame that followed stung, but not badly. I fed the new spark with the power in my core and grew slightly.

"Whoa, I didn't know you could do that!" he said, eyeing my hand.

I pulled the power back in myself. I had to stifle a shiver at the new spark. It was a delicious feeling, nearly erotic. Kind of like that feeling when you go over a small bump in a car. It made things go all tingly.

"Sometimes starting this way may be a little easier," I said.

He placed his hand between us and smirked. "Light me up, baby."

"Okay, as soon as you feel the flame in your palm, pull on your core, but not a lot. It should stay in your hand then you can add to the flame from your well," I instructed, holding the lighter.

I held the lighter against his palm and flicked it on. The flame danced in his palm for a moment and then he caught it with his power. His eyes went wide at it, but he held steady. I smiled at him.

"Great job! Now, pull everything back into your core."

He concentrated on the small ball of fire and then it faded to an ember then disappeared. A shiver wracked his body.

"Holy fucking hell. That felt amazing," he said, smiling. His eyes darted behind me for a moment then returned.

"Again?" I asked, also grinning.

His jaw slackened and his eyes went wide at something just over my shoulder. Had he set my hair on fire? My hand went to my head, patting it down.

That would be my luck. I turned around to see what had him so shocked.

The world stopped. The slight breeze that had the leaves swaying slightly, halted. The sounds of distant cars vanished. The pink haze from the setting sun faded. My heartbeat sped up. Even the sounds of my rushing blood and erratic pulse were gone. The world may have very well stopped turning. It was me and him. It would always be that way. I was in shock. Maybe it wasn't him, maybe it was some cosmic joke.

At seeing him, my hand flew to cover my heart, as though I could stop it from bursting in my chest. How? When? My thoughts were flooding me with questions, and I tried to grab on the edge of something.

"Delaney," Reid whispered in a low, controlled tone. He said it as though he was coaxing an injured deer.

My vision blurred.

I did the only thing I could. I let go of the edge, and I ran to him.

REID JAMISON

TEN

I SCENTED HER before I ever saw her. The scent of ozone and gardenias wafted the air, and my heart felt as though it was being pulled in a direct line to her. Getting here hadn't been easy. Little money and no identification made for slow travel. I was surprised to see her back facing me. Her plump little ass and hips, my cock twitched just at the sight of her. I was frozen in her presence. I couldn't seem to make my feet move a single step closer to her. Just what was I afraid of? For the second time in my life, I was afraid. I was afraid of how she would look at me. Fuck afraid, I was terrified. This female. This girl held all of me in her palm, to do with as she wished.

I closed my eyes and took a deep breath. When I opened, them, I saw her turning toward me. My heart stopped and my breathing grew ragged. I nearly went to my knees. Her hand covered her heart as though the sight of me pained her. I took a small step toward her, but stopped myself. I needed her to come to me. I didn't know why it was so important, but it was.

Oh, hell no. I couldn't cause her anymore pain. The words of the god in my dream hit me, "…she is breaking." Had she already broken?

"Delaney," I whispered in a soft coaxing tone. My whole world narrowed to one single point. One single moment. Her and right now. She ran to me and oh, how the searing pain of the last few months seemed to ebb. The tears that streamed down her face fell from her cheeks like small falling stars. Then she was in my arms, her damp face buried in my chest. Nothing in my life had ever felt so certain. Right now, with this female, I felt as though I was where I should have always been.

I felt her softly trembling. Wait, no, sobbing. I pulled her tighter to me. We sank to the ground. Right where we stood. In front of this rickety old house, for everyone to see. I pulled her onto my lap, pressed my face into her hair and inhaled. Her scent assailed me. She smelled of home. She was muttering something I couldn't understand. I tried to pull back so I could better hear her, but she clung to me. My heart swelled at that simple action. Then I finally caught what she was uttering.

"Real. You can't be real." Over and over between gasps of air.

"Shh, baby, I'm very real and very here," I murmured to her. Her small form thrummed with energy. With every gasp and sob she sent a jolt of electricity through me. I steeled myself against the pain of each pulse of her power. *Has she gotten stronger?*

I clutched her closer and ran a hand down her head, smoothing her hair and cooing to her. I told her how much I missed her. I told her that I would never let her go. I told her everything. I held nothing back from her. Belatedly, I realized she had gone still in my arms. This time, when I pulled back from her, she allowed it. I peered down at her face. Her gray gaze was glowing silver. Her eyes were puffy and rimmed with red. Her lips were swollen. I brushed a finger along her mouth and shuddered at the feel of her. Those lips. They were my drug and salvation. I dipped my head lower and brushed my lips against hers. I couldn't stop myself from taking her mouth in pure abandon.

She responded to me so sweetly, meeting me with equal need. Our tongues met, and there we sat, tasting each other as though we were consuming each other. My shaft stiffened beneath her, and I shifted her. As I did, my stiffness ground against her, and she gasped. I growled in response.

"Uh, so how about we get the two of you in the house? As much as I love a show and won't protest at all if y'all go at it, I don't need the neighbors calling asking about the white people making out on the lawn." Troy's voice seemed to crash through the fog in my muddled head.

I pulled my lips from Delaney's and rested my forehead against hers. We both sat there for a few moments, panting. I couldn't get enough of her. I wanted to consume all of her. I begrudgingly shifted her off of me and stood up, pulling her with me.

"How?" she questioned in a hoarse voice.

"Let's get inside. I'll tell you everything."

The house smelled of fire and smoke. I raised an eyebrow at Troy and he shrugged in response. Then I felt it. Troy had power. A lot of power. I hadn't felt this from him in the past. My eyes went wide. He felt like a witch. I tried to wrack my brain to recall if he had ever felt like this before. All I wanted to think about was the soft female I held onto.

We walked up the stairs to a small, yet lavishly decorated room.

"I'll let you two be," Troy said, closing the door.

"Troy wait," I called after him.

He paused and turned to me. I kissed Delaney on the forehead and pulled away from her. After a moment she let me go. I walked over to Troy and hugged him.

"Thank you. For being there for her when I wasn't." My words were choked with pain and regret. He hugged me back.

In a tone full of emotion, Troy said, "She's my family." He pulled away and wiped at his cheeks. "Making me cry. Now I have to go touch up my makeup." He walked away shaking his head.

I turned to face the woman sitting on the bed. She bit her bottom lip and looked so vulnerable. I had to pinch myself, praying this wasn't another dream. I walked over to her and sat down, pulling her to me. We sat there, just holding one another, for what seemed to be hours.

"How?" Her voice washed over me, lighting just about every nerve on fire.

I told her about where I was taken, about how I thought she was dead until Mitch came, about the dream, about the coin, and about the escape on the new moon. I told her everything. She sat there listening, yet not responding. I hoped she was just numb with emotion. I put my hands on either side of her face and cradled her.

"I'm here now and I'm not going to hold anything back from you. Not one thing, Delaney."

She closed her eyes, clearly trying not to cry. But soon tears streamed down her cheeks. Each tear seemed to flash and spark as it fell.

"Look at me," I crooned to her.

She opened her beautiful gray eyes.

"I need you to see me when I tell you this next bit," I said, trying to keep my voice steady. I took a deep breath and said the one thing I needed to say to her. The one thing that my heart had been screaming from the moment she ran into me.

"I love you, Delaney. And I'll keep you." I couldn't keep my feelings out of my voice. It pulsed with every syllable. My emotion seemed to give the words a heartbeat and breath. They were now a living breathing thing.

"I love you, too." Her voice was a whisper. With her words, an emotion flashed across her face. Doubt? I was taken aback. I frowned down at her.

"What's wrong?" I was slightly panicked. I'd just given her my heart and soul.

"What …" She paused as though she was trying to choke out the next words. "What did Mitch tell you?" Her scent hit my nose again and I smelled a scent I did not think I would ever get from her, not with me. Fear. Why was she afraid? I told her everything he told me. Her face lost all of its color and she wouldn't look at me. I became racked with panic. Just what had Mitch done to her?

"Delaney, tell me what happened."

She refused to meet my eyes. I put a finger under her chin and coaxed her to look at me. She looked so defeated. Her expression nearly broke me.

"Reid, please, I don't want you to think worse of me." Even her tone was defeated.

"Delaney, I could never have anything other than love for you. Please tell me." I tried to keep my tone even, but I was writhing with hatred for Mitch. I didn't want Delaney to think it was toward her.

Then she told me everything. She told me how he made her hunt and that she actually enjoyed the running, but that the killing unnerved her. That made me smile as I too enjoyed it. Then she told me the rest. She told me how he kept her locked up. Then she told me of the two times she tried to escape. The beatings, though I could feel she was holding back some details. I wouldn't push her, not when she was so open with me. Then she told me how she allowed him to touch her in order to escape.

He had abused her. My beautiful Delaney had been hurt in ways I couldn't fathom. I had two very distinct feelings. First, was loathing. I loathed Mitch and my resolve to see him not only dead, but ripped to teeny tiny bits, strengthened. And second, was unimaginable pain. My heart felt like it died painfully, slowly with each word. He had hurt her, and I wasn't there to help her. She was trembling with each utterance. I pulled her closer to me. She softened into me ever so slightly. *I may not have been there to save her, but I'm here now, and I WILL put her back together.*

She couldn't meet my eyes when she said, "I feel dirty and used. I'm so disgusted with myself." Her words felt like a vice tightening around my chest. I have never been good with words, but right now I needed to say something to her and it had never been so important that I get it right.

"Delaney, I wish you could see yourself the way I see you." My voice was strained, nearly hoarse. She looked away in shame. *Shit. I fucked it up.* I grasped her chin between my finger and thumb and coaxed her face up so I could see her and her me.

"You would see a woman who has been through so much pain and loss. You would see a beautiful woman who is so strong and vibrant that she will come out of the other side glowing. You're not dirty. The one thing you are, is mine." I took a deep breath, readying myself to ask her the one thing that I had been needing to from the first moment.

"I want you beyond this life. I want you longer than forever. I want you to be my mate." My heart was hammering against my chest. Her reply was more than important; it was everything. It was what I needed to make it past this moment. She sat there blinking at me and not saying anything. Her eyes flickered from gray to glowing silver and back again.

"But I'm broken." It was the barest whisper.

I pursed my lips. "Well, it's a good thing I'm great at fixing things."

She finally met my eyes. In them was the one emotion that nearly caused me to jump up on the bed and cry to the stupid gods with joy. It was hope. I could work with hope. She threw her arms around my neck and I pulled her on my lap and shifted her so she was straddling me. She tucked her face into my neck. Her heart beat against my chest like a wild horse.

After several moments she said, "I want to be your mate. I don't really know what that means though."

My heart swelled. I smiled at her. I cradled her face in my hands and pulled her lips to mine, falling in love with her all over again. She tasted so sweet I could drink her in. Her soft little lips parted slightly, and her wicked little tongue darted out to lap at mine. It drove me near the edge of my control. I stiffened under her drugging little mouth and pulled away. She was panting softly, and the air was filled with the scent of her arousal. It fanned my own to a near fever pitch.

"This is more than a marriage. This bond, Delaney, will go beyond this life. This binds our souls together." I wanted to be sure this was what she wanted.

Without hesitation she said, "Good." I couldn't help but smile back at her.

"But what do I need to do?" Her tone was cautious.

"Well," I said, bringing my face close to her ear. I kissed the smooth skin of her soft neck. She shivered. "First, I'm going to get you wet and ready for me." I darted my tongue out and licked the same spot I kissed. Again her body trembled in response. "Then, I'm going to bite you right here." I nipped her. Her breaths came quicker. "And when I bite you, Delaney,

I'm going to be so deep inside of you, you won't know where you end and I begin." My shaft was so hard at that point it was nearing painful. She shifted slightly and a jolt of pleasure shot through me, causing me to growl in her ear. A small whimper escaped her lips.

"Then what?" she asked in a husky tone.

"Your beast will guide you, Delaney. You need to let her," I said as I began to run a hand up and down her side. When I got to the swell of her breast, her breath hitched. God, I knew I needed to go slow with her, but my beast was screaming for me to take her and take her hard.

She shifted again, grinding her sex against my rock hard erection, and I nearly tossed her to the bed. I raised a hand to cup her breast. Her nipple was hard against the material of her shirt. I wanted nothing more at that moment than to tongue her pebbled flesh. She arched into my hand, pressing herself more fully into my palm.

"Reid! Delaney! There's someone here asking for you." Troy's voice seemed to break a spell. I could have killed him.

She was the one who growled this time. Then his words broke through the mental fog. *Someone is here? Shit, Mitch!* I stood up, causing Delaney to topple to the floor. Damn.

"Sorry," I said, offering her a hand. She took it and ran out the door and down the stairs. She clearly had the same thought I did, because I could smell the scent of ozone trailing after her.

ELEVEN

I PULLED LIGHTNING to my palms and raced down the stairs. I'd only been this Witch/werewolf hybrid for a few months and these scenes were a little new to me. My brain did not connect the dots that my nose had provided. I nearly plowed right through Troy, but stopped just short. His eyes went wide at the sparks falling from my hands. Then he put his hands on his hips and narrowed his gaze at me.

"What are you? The fucking welcoming committee? Dial it back there, killer. Take it from kill to stun, would you?" He had a look of horror on his face.

I stood there blinking at him. I reluctantly pulled my lightning back to my core. I felt a strong arm snake

53

around my waist. I knew it was him, but I still stiffened. He shuddered at the residual charge left covering my skin. I still couldn't believe what he had done to get to me. My thoughts slid back to everything I had done and had let happen to me. *How could he still want me? Why would he?*

Then Reid did something that shocked me right out of my own head. He moved the hand that was wrapped around my waist to my face and he booped my nose. He actually put his finger up and tapped my nose. The gesture caught me so off guard I nearly stuttered.

In my ear he whispered, "You need to learn to use this thing."

Did he really just boop me? I stood there blinking in shock. This werewolf, who was about as big as a truck, as manly as could be, just booped me. Then both his action and meaning hit me. I was ignoring what my nose was telling me all along: it wasn't Mitch. I didn't know who the hell it was; it wasn't him though. I tried to relax, but as of late I was finding that increasingly difficult to do.

"It's Monique. From the Coven. I asked her to come," Reid said, reluctantly letting me go. *Yeah, me too.* This was the witch I happened to call on the phone. We walked into the living room that was just across the walkway from the kitchen. There, standing in the middle of the cozy room, was a tall African American woman. My jaw nearly hit the floor with how stunningly beautiful she was. She wasn't created, she was crafted, or maybe even painted. Each angle of her face seemed to be a swipe of a brush rather than the edge of a bone. Her hair was absolutely magnificent. It was wildly natural and had streaks of gold. She looked like a queen. I instantly hated her. Okay, no, but wow, she was pretty.

"Hey, Earth to Spock." Troy's voice broke through my mental barrier.

"Yeah, sorry, phasers set to stun, I know. Glad to hear you're finally watching Star Trek," I said, flashing him a smile. I hadn't realized I missed smiling so damned much. I guess it felt foreign because in the past few months, I did it so little. A little piece of normal was inching its way back into my life and damn it I was going to hold on to it with every ounce of strength in my body.

"Hey, don't go telling everyone. I have a reputation to maintain."

I returned my attention to Monique Thomas, the stunning Earth witch standing mere feet from me. It made me more than a little nervous to have such a powerful Witch this close to me, but her being part to the inner circle of the Coven made me even more on edge. Reid walked over to the woman and proceeded to hug her. Then I heard a low growl. I looked around only to realize it had come from me. Oops. *Feeling a little possessive are we? Hell yes, I am. I only just got him back.* Troy elbowed me in the ribs.

"Sorry." Yeah, I wasn't a bit sorry.

"You lie like a rug." He knew me well.

Reid raised an eyebrow at me and I just shrugged. I walked over and stuck my hand out to her in greeting.

"Hi, I'm Delaney. You must be Monique."

She grabbed my outstretched hand, as soon as our skin met, she withdrew quickly. "Ouch," she said as she cradled her hand.

I winced. Dammit. I hated hurting people I didn't mean to. "Sorry."

She eyed me then, a dazzlingly white smile slashing her dark face. She stepped closer and reached her hand out again.

I eyed it, not really understanding what she wanted.

"May I?" she questioned.

I had no clue what she wanted. I raised my eyebrow at her then shrugged. She stepped closer and placed her hand just over my heart. That's when I realized what she was doing. When I meet a witch, it's easy, for the most part, to gauge their power level based on the thrum of power they are giving off. But touching them just over the heart will give an accurate feel for just how much power they have. When I did this to Troy, I pegged him for a nine, easy. Though I wouldn't tell him that. His ego would inflate his head and then he wouldn't be able to fit through doorways. There was a risk of letting a witch so close to you though. She could make one small pulse of power and boom, as Troy would say, dead. The one benefit I would have in this situation was that I could, in turn, gauge her power.

There was a small spark of power when she touched me. But the spark grew. It should have dissipated. I focused on her power. It felt like Earth, like being rooted to the ground. Her file said she was at a power level of a nine. It lied. She was a ten. Her power was so strong I was willing to bet she found mine to be a trickle compared to her ocean. I opened my eyes to see her mouth gaping in shock.

"Did I do something wrong?" I asked, biting my lip.

She removed her hand and eyed me before saying, "No, Delaney, I just wasn't expecting that."

My heart sank to my feet. Not that it mattered how much power I had, but her look made me feel insubstantial.

She saw my fallen expression and quickly added, "No, Delaney, you misunderstand. I have never felt any witch have as much power as you. On the scale of one to ten that we use, Delaney, you're twenty at least. I-I don't even know how to quantify it."

I just stood there blinking at her. That couldn't be correct. It just couldn't. Mil had done this with me after puberty and said I was an eight.

I shook my head and explained, "No you need to try again. Mil said I was an eight."

"Delaney, the power that I felt was more than I have ever felt in anyone. Ever."

"Your file said you were a nine. That was a lie. You're a ten easy." A look of shock flashed across her face then it settled into resignation.

"Bernard is the one who assesses all of the inner circles power levels. He does not do well with competition. It doesn't surprise me in the least that he lied. It's nice to know though." My head was spinning. I mean I thought I had some power, but that much power? I didn't think I could wrap my head around it.

"D, you did that thing to me; what's my power level?" Troy questioned brightly.

I sighed and mumbled, "Nine."

"I couldn't understand that, try getting the dick …"

"Oh my God, Troy! You're a nine. Same as Mil was," I said, trying to cut off his words.

"Hell yes, bitches! I'm like a superhero." And there it was. *Insert ego inflation here.*

"Now, if you can stop burning shit down," I quipped.

"I know, I know. But, this is all new to me. I could turn Reid here into Pam Anderson, with nothing but blush and some spackle. I'm the fucking MacGyver of drag queens. But this shit is way out of my purview."

"New?" Monique asked Troy with a confused expression pinching her eyes.

I explained what I thought happened with Mil and Troy.

"Well, it's possible. She would have needed a lot of power though. Like you, I thought it was a myth."

Then I realized I had a lot of questions for her.

"Not to be mean, but why are you here? I mean other than Reid asking." My hands flew to my mouth. *I did not just ask that? Shut up, Delaney!* Apparently, my brain to mouth filter was on the fritz.

"Damn, D."

I rolled my eyes at Troy.

"I'm here to help, but I'm also here for a few other reasons." We all made our way to the couches to hear just what she had to say.

"Okay, when you called, I tried to tell you just what the Coven has been doing, you just hung up too fast," she said.

I shivered at the memory of what happened after that phone call. My ribs ached slightly, just recalling it. I pushed the memories back and tried to focus on her words.

"The Coven started a breeding program a few years ago. They have found a way to breed more witches. They are forcing it on the witches on the reservations. They are brainwashing them and if that doesn't work, they are threatening them. I knew they were trying to breed more witches, but God, I never thought that this was even a possibility, much less a reality. They breed them, then take the children. If the children have power, they are kept. God, Delaney, the ones that don't, I-I don't know what happens to them." Her eyes shimmered with unshed tears.

I was horrified. I think we all were, because no one could speak. The thought that they were forcing witches to breed like cattle, then the children are taken, and God knows what happens if they didn't have power, made bile rise up and splash the back of my throat. I'd always been afraid of the Coven. Always running and trying to hide from them. Screw that. I'm done hiding from them. They want me? They can come and get me. It said in the prophecy I would take them down. Well, I didn't need some prophecy to tell me that. It was fact. My vision wavered from color to black and white.

"Delaney, calm down." It was a distant voice, but a familiar one. I blinked, and the color slowly returned.

"Sorry." My voice was raspy.

"That's just so amazing. You were sparking over your whole body," Monique commented with a look of awe.

I looked down at my clothes that were still smoking. I saw about a dozen tiny holes burned into the fabric. *Shit.*

"Great, now I'm going to have a Delaney-sized ass print burned in my couch."

"Monique, I want to help and I'm sure we all do, but Mitch is a problem we need to deal with," Reid explained, pulling me closer against him. I breathed in his scent. It was a mix of sandalwood and pine. It seemed to center me and bring my wild emotions back down.

"I want him dead." My tone was cold and emotionless. I'd never in my life needed someone to die. They all looked at me. I had no more fucks to give. They could think me a monster if they liked. I wouldn't lie.

"Me too," Monique added with a stony expression. Now that took me aback. She went on and told us just how she was connected to Mitch. I listened to every word. It had been her. That's how Mitch found out about the prophecy. She had never meant for him to hear, but it had been her. She couldn't meet my eyes as she spoke. I tried to be mad at her. I tried to blame her for all that had happened, but I couldn't. She had loved Mitch, and he used her like yesterday's underpants.

I flopped back on the couch. There was so much here. *So many variables in this.* Then I had this niggling question in the back of my mind. I looked fully at Monique and voiced the question as evenly as I could.

"I understand you want to help us with Mitch. That I understand. I guess I don't get why you would leave your position at the inner circle of the Coven to help us bring them down."

An emotion flashed across her face, though I had no idea what it was. Annoyance maybe, or even anger. Her face then went hard when she said, "Because what they are doing is deplorable. They are all following Bernard without question, and it's not right. I won't have this on my conscience."

She seemed sincere, but there was something I couldn't place. Maybe her tone or the way her full, bowed mouth strained around her words. Something I didn't trust. Then again, after the shit I'd been through, I didn't trust myself, much less anyone else. I would have to keep my eye on her; I couldn't turn down help at this point though. We needed all the help we could get.

Why did this have to be so complicated? Why did I have to be in the middle of any of it? I could just take Troy and Reid and run off to Amsterdam. We could open a little bakery and coffee shop. Yeah, maybe I would have to learn to cook for that mess. I sighed.

Well, when in doubt ask yourself WWSD. What would Spiderman do? I closed my eyes and tried to picture the superhero. The only thing I could picture were the words, "With great power comes great responsibility." I groaned because I knew I couldn't run. I owed it to Sierra, Mil and the rest of the witches Mitch destroyed before he found me.

"Welp, what do we do now?" It was Troy who broke the tense silence.

I lifted my head off the back of the plush couch and looked at the three other people in the room. There were four of us. Four people. Two witches, one werewolf, and me, whatever I was. How could so few of us take down not only Mitch, but get through his whole pack to get to him?

"I think Monique needs to teach Troy about how to control his power. And I want to take you out and teach you what I can about being a wolf," Reid said, squeezing my thigh.

"I don't think we have that much time. I mean, Mitch will come for me. It won't take him too long to figure out where I am. It's not like I had too many places I could have gone." *We are so, so, so, screwed.*

God, I just hoped we found some lube by the time he came for us, to make said fucking less painful. We needed something, a break, anything.

"I think we have a few days at least. Mitch will most likely go north. I mean he would think you would come to me. He would have no idea we were already here," Reid said, though I don't think he believed his own words.

"What about calling another pack?" The rest of the packs, if they knew what Mitch had done, should be willing to help right? Maybe I was grasping at straws here. I didn't know what else to do.

Reid looked grim. "I could try to call some of them, but there is so much disorganization among the packs that I doubt they would be willing to help. They tend to be of the mind that if it's not in their backyard then they don't need to get involved. And they also don't take kindly to a lone wolf pleading a pack for help to attack another pack." My last little bit of hope fell. I hadn't realized I held that much hope out.

Troy cleared his throat as though to interject. I raised an eyebrow at him. Was he asking permission? Who was this person and what happened to the queen who questioned no one. I guess Garrett had a calming effect on him.

"Look, I haven't been a witch for that long, and I don't know shit all about anything. Well, unless you want me to turn Reid here into a woman …"

He was rambling. I motioned for him to get on with it. But his words did make me smile.

"Sorry. What I'm trying to say is, Delaney is a bad bitch. And God knows I'm a bad bitch. Monique here seems like a bad bitch and Reid…" He trailed off, eyeing Reid. He then added, "Well I think you get where I'm going with that. We are a group that one does not simply fuck with. Why don't we just go the hell up there with our badassness and fuck 'em up."

Just as I was about to open my mouth to say something, my cell phone rang. It was the phone Mark had given me before I left. My mouth went dry, and my heartbeat went to supersonic speeds. Who the hell could be calling me? I fished the phone out of my pocket. It was an Atlanta number as it had a 770 area code. I glanced at Reid. He seemed as alarmed as I was. It was on the third ring. I accepted the call and held the device to my ear.

"Um, hello?" My voice was shaky. *Way to answer a phone, Delaney*.

"Hello? Is this Delaney?" It was a female voice, and she was upset and rushed.

"Yes. Who is this?"

"This is Kate. Mark's wife." My heart went from supersonic to nothing. All noise died, and the people, scent, and activity in the room paused. *God, please let Mark be okay.* I was ignoring what my brain was telling me, what my heart was telling me.

"I-I got a call from Mitch and …" She paused, choking on a sob. My throat tightened. I had to tighten down these emotions. "… He said I was soon to be a widow and then hung up."

And it was all because of me. One more person who wanted to help me would pay the price. Okay, it was time to end this *woe is me* shit. I swallowed the tears I knew wanted to be shed and clamped down on everything but my mind.

"Kate, you need to get out of the city. You need to run."

"Mark told me to run the night of the new moon. I-I don't know how to breathe without him." I could hear her tears. A vice tightened around my heart and I thought it might explode with pain. "Mark told me to call you if I didn't hear from him. He gave me a number to give you and wanted me to tell you to call Anderson. He refused to tell me more."

"Okay, what's the number?" My voice was tight, but I wouldn't cry. Hell, I wasn't even sure I had any more tears left. She relayed the number to me, and I committed it to memory.

"Delaney, kill him. You kill Mitch and make it hurt." Her tone turned cold and steady. It was as though this deed, this one action was the only driving force she had.

"Kate, I'll rip him apart." My tone was just as cold. She hung up and at that moment I knew I would. I would kill him. Maker or not. I was never very good at following the rules anyway.

DELANEY HAGEN
TWELVE

MONIQUE AND TROY went out to the backyard to practice, and by practice I mean Monique was holding a fire extinguisher and Troy was screaming about burning his eyebrows off. The poor guy was going to have to watch some YouTube videos about drawing on eyebrows because from what I've seen, Troy was in a constant state of shock. Not a good look for anyone.

Reid and I went back to the bedroom. He told Monique and Troy that we had pressing business to attend to. I turned thirty-six shades of red and Troy just smiled. As much as I loved Reid and gods knows I did, I needed to call Anderson.

No sooner did that bedroom door close behind him when he said, "Call him."

I raised an eyebrow at him and gave him a shy smile. *Silly man, he thought he needed to tell me that.* I sat down and dialed the number.

"Anderson." His voice was nice. It was low, with a slight southern drawl.

"Um, hi …"

"Don't speak." He cut me off, and I was so shocked, my mouth just gaped at the phone.

I pulled the phone from my ear to be sure I dialed the correct number. I had. I returned to the phone to hear muffled voices and rustling. I caught Reid eyeing me. I shrugged.

"Okay, I know who this is." My eyes went wide. *He knew? How?*

"This was Mark's phone. He would only give it to one person."

"Okay, Kate called me and told me to call you. Is he …" I trailed off, not wanting to ask the question for fear of it coming to fruition.

"Not yet. Mitch is ... playing with him." I could hear the disgust in his voice. But it didn't feel right. Like he was putting it on.

"Why did he want me to call you?" That was the question I needed answered before all others.

"The pack isn't behind Mitch. He has about ten that are staunch supporters. But that's it." This could be what we needed, a way in without the pack getting in the way. Or he could be lying.

"Okay."

"Mitch is going south to find you, but he's waiting until the full moon. He wants to be as strong as possible. He won't have the support of the pack. Though we won't back you, we won't stand in your way either."

His tone was even. He sounded as though he was absolutely resolute in this decision.

"I'm not sure I understand."

"Mitch is taking about twenty wolves down there. Half of them are mine. They won't fight with Mitch. Not after what he has done to Mark. We won't aid you. Just know you have eleven wolves after you, not the whole pack."

"Why won't you help me if you're going against Mitch?"

"He's our maker. And we will never follow a witch. This is as much as we are willing to do for you. For protecting Mark. You have two weeks. Get ready." The line clicked then went dead.

"You don't believe that bullshit, do you?" Reid asked, taking the phone from me and crushing it in his hand.

"Hey, why did you do that? And not a chance in hell."

"It was Mark's. No need to give them a way to pinpoint our location." Good point.

"What now?" I asked, staring up into Reid's hot caramel gaze. I could get lost in their depths. I let my eyes travel down his face to settle on his full mouth. I remembered how his lips tasted and the talented tongue that lay inside. I was growing damp, and a delicious throb began to build between my legs. Would he still want me? After everything? I wanted to kick myself for even asking that question. I tried to push the self-destructive thoughts out of my mind so I could focus on the man in front of me. His eyes sparked with desire, and his scent was spiked with an addictive quality.

He reached for my face. I had to stifle a flinch. I hated that I had that kind of reaction to Reid. It wasn't him; it was freaking Mitch. It was how he forced me to take his touches. It was how he beat me. It was what I had to do to get out of there. I pushed the thoughts aside and tried once again to focus on my Reid.

In a motion that was nearly identical to a predator pouncing on its prey. Reid descended upon my lips in a kiss filled with such longing and erotic need that it would leave me panting; that was if he let me go long enough. He was famished, and I was what he needed and I reveled in it. Who needed breath anyway, right? Breathing wasn't necessary with this man. His tongue teased mine with quick short laps, and his teeth nipped my lip. It took me a moment to realize that as he was obliterating my mind, he was moving me back toward the bed. My ass hit the mattress and it seemed to shock me out of the spell he was casting.

I pulled away from him just long enough to take in a much-needed gulp of air. My heart was racing like a wild thing. His eyes blazed green with his growing arousal and need. That flicker, that blaze of green, caused my heart to beat even faster. He lifted me up on the bed.

His head ducked down to the base of my throat. Right where my pulse was fluttering. He gave it a small lick, and I shivered at the contact. I let a sigh slip out, just as I grasped his shoulders. His right hand trailed from the nape of my neck and headed south. He traced one finger under my ear, down my collar bone, to settle on my left breast. He didn't grab like I expected and braced for, he trailed a finger, tracing circles around it. Both of my nipples puckered in response to him. When he drew a small circle around my pebbled flesh, I sucked in a gulp of air. Then his hand cupped my breast fully. He growled low in his chest in reaction. Liquid heat rushed to my sex, causing me to moan and arch up to him. This man wrecked me. He tore down every wall or barricade I had, leaving me scrambling to pick up the pieces.

He inhaled deeply and moaned huskily, "Take your top off. I want to see you."

I did as he asked. His eyes went wide at the sight of my chest, and a smile quirked his lips upward.

"Cherries?" he questioned with a smile.

"It was all they had," I whispered indigently. I was nervous, and heat spread across my face in a deep blush. There was no call to be shy. He loved me, and I loved him. I was not a blushing virgin anymore. There was no reason to be so scared of him. I closed my eyes as he reached for me again. He dusted light kisses along my throat while he dipped one finger inside my bra to brush my stiffened peak. I felt, more than heard, his steady growls of appreciation as he kissed his way painfully, slowly down my neck.

My body stiffened. What if he could tell? What if he could tell just what Mitch had done to me? What if he could tell what I'd let happen to me? He would find out. I just knew he would. I realized Reid had stopped kissing me and his hands cradled my face. His low voice finally cracked through the fog. I opened my eyes to see him staring at me with concern on his face.

"Delaney, love, what's wrong?" He brushed a thumb over my right cheek.

Am I crying? Great, God I'm so messed up.

"I-I-I don't know." I looked away because I did know. I couldn't do this. I tried to suck in more air. That was what I needed wasn't it?

"Delaney, we don't need to do this right now. Not if you're not ready." His tone was calming. I looked at him, trying to center myself. His tawny hair had grown out slightly and fell over in clumps across his forehead. He tilted his head to mine causing our heads to lean together.

I breathed in his scent, and that seemed to give me the strength I needed to admit the next words, "I think I'm broken."

"Oh, my love. You're not broken. But if you were, you shouldn't worry. I'm here to fix you." His voice held so much love. So much love that I didn't deserve.

"What Mitch did and what I let him ..."

"Stop ..." He lifted his head up and knelt to meet my gaze. "You did nothing wrong. He did. And he will pay. But, love, you can't let this break you. Delaney, you're stronger than that. It's time you figure that out."

God, but he was right. I needed to move past this.

"I want this with you, but I don't think I can do it like this." My words were shaky, but dammit I was ready to move past this fear.

"How do you want me, love?" My heart did a little flip-flop thing at the endearment.

"I think I need to set the pace. You know, be in control." I flushed. I didn't know how to talk about this kind of thing without feeling like a goober. His eyes flicked from caramel to green. Clearly, he was totally game with that idea. He kissed my nose then stood up. His smile went from sweet to wicked. I made a vow to him, a silent one. I wouldn't let my self-doubt or the aftermath of what Mitch had done to me affect how I saw Reid. I wouldn't.

"How do you want me?" he asked in a gruff tone.

"Take your shirt off," I instructed.

He did, but as slowly as possible. His muscles rippled with each move of his arms. Part of me wanted to have him do that again, so I could see his taut stomach tense and his pecks move with his twisting. Someone was panting. *Oh shit, that's me.* His tanned nipples were flat and my mouth watered to lick them. My sex throbbed in time with my wild heartbeat.

"Now what?" His voice was rough and he was trying to let me have control over this situation, but he was an alpha and this was difficult for him. And the fact that he was surrendering to me in this way aroused me to a near fever pitch.

I got up and spoke in a tone that was much huskier than I expected, "Lay on the bed."

He did as instructed. His erection caused his pants to tent and my sex to throb so hard it was nearing on pain. I pulled my shorts off and kicked them to the side. Then I crawled on top of him so that I straddled his thighs.

"God, Delaney, I can smell your heat from here and it's driving me mad." His eyes no longer flickered. They blazed green. I was in control. I wouldn't fear him or this. He was not Mitch.

I unbuttoned his pants. The head of his cock was so swollen with need I nearly lost my control. I pulled the zipper down one notch at a time. By the time I got to the last notch, I realized I was grinding my slick heat against his thigh.

"I can feel how wet you are …" He groaned audibly. "And oh for fuck's sake, Delaney, I'm fighting the urge to drive into you."

His big chest heaved with each breath. He was trembling with the need to touch me. God bless that wolf, he didn't move a finger. His erection was now free and holy hell it was glorious. I could see a small bead of pre-cum on the head and wanted so desperately to lap it up. I shifted off of him only long enough to pull his pants off the rest of the way. I straddled him, and he groaned at the feel of my now dripping sex against his shaft. He could no longer hold himself back. He placed his hands on my hips.

I leaned down and pressed my mouth to his lips. I deepened the kiss by flicking my tongue in and out of his mouth, mimicking the one thing I knew he wanted to be doing. *Silly, predictable wolf.* He moaned into my mouth. I rocked my heated flesh against him. He groaned in response and thrust up. I nearly shouted at the delicious friction. I pulled away and kissed my way to his flat nipples. I licked each one in turn, watching them pebble at the cool air, then shifted my body down him until my lips hovered just above his throbbing shaft. It visibly pulsed. I looked up to him. He was leaning up, to get a better look at me. I wrapped my fingers around him, and his eyes nearly slid shut at the contact.

"What do you want, Reid?" I was playing. Teasing him. This control thing might have been going to my head, but I couldn't help it.

"Oh, Delaney. I … oh God …" He trailed off as I licked the salty bead of his arousal off the head of him.

I smiled up at him and cooed in a sweet voice, "Tell me. What do you want?"

He looked near crazed. He growled, "I want you to lick it again."

Never taking my eyes off him, I licked him again. He shuddered with pleasure. He was salty, with a tang of sweet. I wanted more. I broke our eye contact and slipped the head of him in my mouth. I created a rhythm with my mouth and pumped my hand down his length, because there was no way I could fit all of him in this way. His hips began to thrust upward with each lap and suck. I was nearly dripping wet. My sex was aching. I reached between my legs and dipped my free hand into my panties. I slipped a finger into my sopping folds and found my swollen clit and began stroking it.

He saw the movement and snarled, "I can't do this."

I was so shocked, I stopped, lifting my gaze to his. He grabbed my hips and twisted me until I was straddling his face, leaving my mouth where it started. That was when I understood. He quite literally ripped my panties off.

"Delaney, God, you're nearly dripping."

I was panting. I could feel his cool breath against my super-heated folds. I tried not to whimper. It was a fleeting battle. I was shaking with need.

"Now, little wolf, tell me what you want." Apparently, turnabout was fair play.

"I … oh God … Reid …" I felt his tongue dart out for a fast taste, and it nearly knocked the breath out of me.

Who the hell needed air? What was air again?

"Tell me, Delaney." I felt his hands spread my drenched folds.

I gasped and nearly yelled the words, "I need you to lick me!" I felt his laugh low in his belly, but I was beyond caring. He licked the length of me and I honestly think my vision blurred. I felt him murmur something against me that sounded like "sweet honey," but I was in a different reality. I gave him the same attention he gave to me. He sucked my clit into his mouth and I couldn't hold back a shout. I sucked him into my mouth. This was a game of tit for tat, and oh God, I had no idea who would win. I felt him slide a finger inside of me. *Oh God, he will win. Won? Winning? Oh to hell with grammar.* Where the hell was my white flag?

"You're so tight. I can feel you gripping me," he moaned.

I sucked and licked at him while he fingered and lapped at me. I was beginning to have concentration issues. I felt my peak nearing. I pulled back, because his rhythm was becoming too much for me. I wanted to continue my sensual assault of him, but he had my number and he was calling it in.

"Reid, I can't keep …" I trailed off, as he again sucked my clit into his mouth.

He released me long enough to say, "Come for me." He then licked me harder and slipped a second finger inside of me. I don't know if it was his words or everything else, but it pushed me over the edge. I came in a wet rush. I nearly screamed with the intensity of it. He sucked and lapped up every bit of my orgasm. I tried to pull away, but his wicked fingers only slipped out of me to hold my hips to him. He growled at me. The stimulation was becoming overwhelming and I couldn't take anymore. Finally, sensing this, he released me. I twisted my body until I was facing him. He looked nearly crazed for his own release.

"Take your bra off." His tone was so garbled and rough that I almost couldn't understand him. I reached behind and unclasped it. I let it fall away. This male could only let me have control of the situation for a limited time. It just wasn't in his nature. He groaned in approval. I was growing wet again. I shifted so his shaft was nestled right in my cleft. His cock felt nearly superheated against me. He bucked his hips at the contact.

I leaned down to whisper in his ear, "I'm going to fuck you so hard." He bucked again at my words and his eyes grew even wilder. I slid my sex along his length, gasping at the friction that was oh so electric.

For the briefest moment our bodies aligned and he nudged at my entrance. I moaned at the feeling and he snarled. His hands cupped my breasts.

He found the stiffened peaks and rolled them between his thumbs and forefingers. I sucked in a breath and nearly sobbed with the pleasure of it. I shifted slightly and felt the head of him breech me slightly again. This time, instead of moving away, I slid on to him, impaling myself with his length, inch by aching inch. After what had to be the most agonizing hour, he was fully inside of me. It didn't hurt as much as it stretched me in a way that made me rock on him.

He grasped my hips and growled, "So tight." He was so hot inside of me I just knew we would combust with the friction. One tiny spark and we would go up in flames. He withdrew slightly and then positioned up. The breath whooshed out of me and he shouted with pleasure. I leaned forward and rode his length. It started slow; what had been teasing him, grew to madden me. I needed him deep and was growing crazed. He seemed to sense my distress and thrust up every time I needed him to. I was getting so close to my climax; I couldn't seem to stop myself. The build of my peak left me feeling in a frenzy, a quivering ball of nerves. I didn't want this to end.

He pulled my hand from his chest and looked at me. Something was about to happen. Something that felt so right. He kissed the underside of my wrist. Then he licked it. I shivered. It was such a simple gesture that didn't look erotic, oh sweet God this was Reid. He could make reading the phone book feel sexy.

Against my skin he growled, "Mine. From this moment on. From this life on. Forever mine." This felt like ritual and felt like it deserved an answer.

"Yours. From this life on. Forever yours." I had no idea if what I said was … He sank his teeth into the flesh. Hard. Had his fangs lengthened? I screamed at first in pain, but then, God help me, it hurled me into the most intense orgasm of my life. I only distantly recall feeling the trickle of my warm blood flowing down my arm. I felt his shaft jerk in response to my clenching sheath. The air grew thick with what felt like my magic, but it wasn't. I felt something snap in place at this moment. I could pay little attention to it though. I needed to be here with him at this moment. This moment that felt so soul-blisteringly important.

I ground my sex against him and couldn't stop myself from writhing atop him. He threw his head back and yelled my name as he came. I felt him spurt each hot jet inside of me, filling me, and I reveled in it. I was shivering in the intensity of this moment with him. Finally, the intensity ebbed. My muscles turned to Jell-O and I collapsed on him. We lay there for several moments. I wasn't sure what had just happened, but speech was so far beyond anything I could manage.

I rested my head on his chest and tried to calm with the sound of his booming heartbeat. What the hell just happened? I knew he said he would bite me, but having an orgasm from it? Yeah, I was totally not prepared to have to pick up the former pieces of myself quite like that. I felt like I could take in a full breath of air now. There was no burn to it.

His arms slid around me and he gripped me to him.

"You're mine now. Not just in this life. Forever, you're mine," he murmured in my ear. His breath tickled the hairs near my ear, causing me to shiver.

"You're just as much mine, wolf. Remember that."

I lay atop him simply trying to bring myself down from this. I didn't even know what to call it. Mating? Seemed too primal. Sex? Didn't quite cover it. I rested my head on his chest and he drew light circles on my back. His heart had calmed to a more normal rhythm. The steady beating lulled me to close my eyes.

I'd just dozed when Reid shifted me off of him to lay me on the bed. I growled at him in protest. He got up and I rolled to face him. I blinked up at him.

"I'll be right back." He kissed me on the nose and walked off to the bathroom. His ass moved in such a way that nearly left me panting. As soon as he returned, I got up and went to the bathroom myself to clean up. When I returned, he was sitting on the bed still nude.

I licked my lips and he snarled, "Keep licking those sweet lips with that wicked little tongue and I'm going to do more to you."

I sauntered over until I stood right in front of him only a few inches apart. I licked my bottom lip slowly. His eyes tracked the motion just like the predator he was. He then seized my hips and pulled me to straddle him. His hand fisted in my hair and he pulled my head back, exposing my throat to him. His heated lips brushed my pulse point and then his slick tongue followed. My eyes slid shut and a moan slipped out before I could stop it.

Wait! I had questions. Didn't I? I couldn't think with him this close to me. My body was already responding to him. It was preparing for round two without discussing it with me. Okay, well, let's be honest, I wasn't protesting too hard.

"Wait," I replied in a raspy voice.

He paused, waiting for me to explain. Why had I stopped him again? He released his hold on my hair and finally I was able to think.

"What does this all mean?" I asked, breathlessly. I glanced down at my inner wrist. There was a deep bite wound that did not seem to be healing.

He lifted my hand up to inspect it. A look of pure male satisfaction was plastered across his face as he lightly kissed the wound.

"We are mated. If you're in pain or distress, I'll be able to feel it. And if I am, you will feel it."

"Had your fangs lengthened? You bit me really hard," I questioned. I was so curious about all of this.

"They did. It's in response to you and your willingness. Had I tried to force you, your inner beast would have not whispered the words you needed to say and my body wouldn't have responded."

Interesting. So, Mitch could have never forced a mating with me. Thank God it never got to that point. I had to stifle a shudder at the disgusting thought of him.

"Will it heal?" I asked, looking at my arm again.

He crooked a finger under my chin and drew my gaze to his.

"No. Not like it would had it been a normal injury. It will always look like a fresh scar." He searched my eyes as he spoke. He was looking for some sort of reaction. Horror maybe? He wouldn't find it. I wanted to wear his mark.

"Was that the magic I felt? It felt like my magic, but it wasn't. Then it felt like something snapped into place."

His brow furrowed and he had a questioning look on his face when he replied, "The snap was our mating. I didn't feel any magic though."

I knew I felt magic surge, the air was thick with it. What had it been? He pulled me close to him and we fell back on the bed.

"I love you, but no more questions. Let's sleep."

I nodded in response. I breathed deeply of his scent and melted into him.

"By the way. When it comes time for it, Troy gets to pick out our bedding," he said low in his chest.

I giggled and closed my eyes. Just before drifting off, I thought about something Reid said. I smiled. I think I'd been broken, but now he was fixing me. He was the only thought I had as I fell into sleep.

REiD JAMiSON

THiRTEEN

THE CURVE OF her naked back. The way her
narrow waist tapered into her luscious hips and her
mouthwatering ass had me in a constant state of
arousal. All this female had to do was look at me and
my cock was so hard if felt like it would explode. Her
soft, even breaths on my chest made my heart swell
with just how much I needed her and how much I
needed to protect her. This meant that I needed to
teach Delaney how to protect herself. In turn, I needed
to teach her how to use her power as a wolf. We had a
lot of work to do, but I was still reluctant to disrupt this
moment for fear of losing all of it. Fear of losing this
perfect serenity with her.

I brushed her hair up into my hand then let the loose strands fall through my fingers in a cascade of silk. When I looked at her, I saw my entire life. I saw how it could end in the blink of an eye. Then my thoughts shifted to all of the damage that had been done by Mitch. My beautiful Delaney was shattered into a million pieces when I got to her because of him. Now, I would find every shard and put her back together, there would be retribution. I knew she didn't tell me everything. But how she reacted to me and the way she cried in her sleep, I knew there was so much more he had done to her. I growled low in my chest.

"Don't growl at me, wolf," she whimpered, burying her face in the crook of my neck.

My chest shook with laughter. I smiled down at her. I couldn't help but smile at her. She did like to poke the wolf.

"My love, we need to get up. I have things I need to show you today."

"Ugh! If you wanted me to get up so early, you shouldn't have woken me up four separate times last night," she grumbled.

I laughed out loud at that. "Delaney, as I recall, it was you who woke me up four times. I was simply helpless to say no to you."

She shifted her hand to tap her chin in thought. "Hmm, did I? Yeah, that was me." She shrugged and plopped her head back on my chest.

Just as I was about to add to my myriad of reasons why we should get up, I felt her little tongue dart out and lap at my nipple. I sucked in a breath. And just like that, I was hard for her.

"Love, as much as I want to bend you over this bed and do deplorable things to you, I want to show you some things and we have limited time." My tone was rough, but I was set on this. She must have sensed the resolution in my voice because she groaned and flopped onto her back.

"I don't wanna get up! You can't make me!" she whined, much like a petulant child would.

I rolled to my side to face her and raised an eyebrow.

Her eyes went wide in alarm and she pulled the cover over her head. "No! No. I know that look, don't you do it!" she cried in a frantic tone.

I reached under the cover and felt around until I touched her side. I gripped her side and tickled her. She screamed and squealed.

Between gasps and laughs she begged, "Okay. Stop. Please."

I stopped and crushed my mouth over hers. She responded so sweetly. Her arousal filled the air and her heart beat wildly under my chest. If we kept going like this, we would surely never leave this bed. I broke the kiss and she whined in protest. *I agree.* Her eyes were glowing silver and when they flickered to her normal storm-cloud gray, they looked like the flash of a lightning strike. And God, it made me insane with need.

"If you don't get up, I'm going to tickle you until you scream." My tone was husky, but she nearly ran out of the bed.

A few moments later I heard the whoosh of the shower. Then she screamed. I shot out of the bed so fast the covers tangled around my feet and I went careening to the floor. With more speed than I knew I had, I righted myself and went charging into the bathroom.

Steam billowed out of the small enclosure. I darted my gaze around and saw Delaney standing in the middle of the bathroom gawking at me.

"What's wrong?" *Who do I need to kill?* My heart was hammering in my chest.

"Uh look at me!" she cried, looking down at her nude body.

My eyes trailed over her. I smiled a knowing smile.

"Oh, I'm so happy you're pleased with yourself! But I look like a cheetah!" She motioned to her breasts and abdomen. They were covered in love bites. I couldn't hide my smile. *Hey, what can I say? I'm pleased.*

Clearly, she was not amused, because she narrowed her eyes at me and said, "You aren't Kenickie and this isn't a Hallmark card!"

"I don't know what you just said."

Who the fuck is Kenickie and am I going to have to kill him?

She gaped at me in disbelief. "How? How have you never seen *Grease*? You're old as dirt. That just isn't possible."

"Get in the shower, woman!" I ordered, then added, "Or I'll add more to my collection."

"OH, COME ON, Reid. I'm never going to learn unless you help," Troy called.

After Delaney and I showered, Troy and Monique asked us to help with some of Troy's training. By "help" they meant I had to be the dummy for target practice.

"Troy, there is no way I'm going to let you shoot a fireball at my head in hopes of hitting an apple. You aren't William Tell!" I held out the apple he handed me.

"Oh, come on! Don't be a pussy!" he yelled over the distance that separated me from the three.

"Hey, you are what you eat. And the answer is still no."

Troy's eyes went wide and both he and Monique whirled to face Delaney. Her mouth hung open in shock and then her face turned so red it was nearing on purple. She jerked her head in my direction. Before I had time to register it, she shot a small ball of lightning at me, causing the apple, held out in my outstretched hand, to explode, covering my forearm in sweet sticky goop.

"Turn off the blush, D, I got no sleep because of the racket you two made last night," Troy said laughing.

Delaney threw her hands up in surrender and turned to stalk away.

I walked to the group.

"Nice shot, love."

She scowled at me, but I didn't mind. Her scowl was cute. Not that I would ever tell her that, as I did not wish to be electrocuted. I wrapped an arm around her waist and pulled her close. I didn't think I would ever get enough of being able to touch her like this.

"What's the plan?" Delaney asked. When we had emerged this morning, we told Troy and Monique about the phone call from Anderson. We all agreed we needed to head the pack off before they got to Savannah. This may not be a big city, but there were a lot of people here. Also, we needed to get the upper hand and surprise them. Now, we just needed to come up with a plan. We could do nothing until Troy had better control of his power and Delaney could control her beast a bit better. That was my plan for today.

"Delaney, we need to go. We have a lot of stuff we need to do."

"I bet you do," Troy said, as he waggled his eyebrows at Delaney.

She slapped him in the stomach.

"Oof, hooker."

"Keys inside?" she asked Troy.

He nodded, giving her the middle finger. She smiled and turned to the house. I paused, mesmerized by the sawing motion of her ass. I licked my lips and ran a hand over my chin. That girl had me wrapped around her little finger.

WE DROVE TO a small clearing that was nestled in some densely wooded areas just off of Highway 17. The trees were so overgrown that there was no way for us to be seen from either the highway or a plane. When I asked Delaney how she knew about this place, her eyes watered slightly. She said there was a stream nearby that opened up into a larger marsh and that she and Sierra came here a number of times.

My woman had been through so much. She had known so much loss, it broke my heart to see it. She solidified her emotions and hardened herself, clearly trying not to show me this vulnerability. *Did Mitch do this to her? Did he harden her?* I growled at the thought. I scented the air. There were the normal woodland smells, but there was a distant scent. It was faint and seemed like it was trying to be masked. I made note of it, then brushed it off. I think my paranoia was getting the best of me.

"Well, master wolf, what now?" she asked.

I smiled at her. "Tell me what Mitch told you about your beast."

"Well, he told me when I change to let it take me over. To give myself over to the thrill of the hunt. The thrill of the kill."

The air between us grew heated and I could scent her excitement just speaking of it.

"Not quite. When you change, you can let the beast out, but you need to keep a leash on it. Mitch lets his beast have far too much control. One of these days, it's going to get him killed."

"Let's hope," she retorted. *Indeed.*

"Mitch barely has control over his wolf. Also, we aren't human, but we aren't wolves either. We are something else. We have attributes of both. Too much of one and that leaves holes and becomes a weakness," I explained.

She nodded, clearly trying to take everything in.

"One of the good things about being mated is I can communicate with you while in wolf form."

Her eyes went wide. Then, her shocked expression turned thoughtful. I quirked an eyebrow at her.

"Well, um, Mitch um …" She trailed off, clearly trying to choose her words carefully.

I tried to swallow back the rage I felt whenever his name fell from her lips. "Go on." I urged.

"Well, he kept pressuring me to mate with him. And then, um, sleep with him. Before I left, he said he would force it on me. I guess if you can't force a mating, why? Why would he want that?"

I had to take a deep breath as not to spew rage everywhere like a wildfire.

"I don't know. Other than him wanting to possess and use you, I don't know."

My tone was harsh. I couldn't help it.

"I'm yours, you know," she whispered, as she put a hand on my shoulder.

I shuddered at the contact and my anger ebbed at her touch. Then a thought struck me.

"Hey, what did that letter from your aunt say?" I had no idea why the thought popped into my head, but there it was.

"Oh shit, I never read it. But, I have it at Troy's," she said, clearly irritated at herself.

"Well, we will worry about it when we get there. Now, I want to see your wolf and how beautiful she is."

She blushed at the compliment, but I knew she wanted to show me. She grabbed the hem of her shirt and pulled it over her head and just like that I was hard for her. I feared I always would be, no matter the situation. I made a mental note to never go to church with her. She stood nude in front of me and I had to fight the urge to fall upon her like a hungry man devouring her inch by sultry inch.

She shook, not because she was cold. Nerves? She took in a deep breath and I went to turn around, knowing how painful a shift as a new wolf could be, but before I could, she shifted. She went from human to wolf as though from one breath to the next. I was in shock at the speed. Never had I ever seen such a smooth and fast shift.

Then I saw her. She was small for a were, but, then again, most females were. She was snow white. Not a single black or tawny hair on her beautiful body. Her body was sleek. She was perfect. She stood about four-and-a-half feet tall and looked as though she wasn't built for brute force, but speed. And her eyes were glowing silver. She was so stunning I had no words. I walked over to her. When I got within a few inches of her, she ducked her head in submission. I sighed and the beast in me stirred. I had a feeling she would look at me as her alpha. I imagined the thought of being an alpha would ruffle, but it didn't.

I wanted to try to communicate with her, but I'd never done this before. I felt around for our mental connect. It took a little while, but I found it.

"Hello, love."

Her ears twitched and then she began pawing at her head, clearly distressed. The beast had the upper hand and I needed her to reign her in.

"Delaney, feel for the connection. Once you find it, you need to find a happy medium with your beast. She can't control you this much. You'll hurt someone," I tried to say aloud in a calming tone.

She was struggling. I knew there was nothing I could do. This was her battle. She had to do this and she would have to face this for a few months before she would have full control in this form. After a few minutes and a few head shakes, she seemed to calm. I tried our mental connection once more.

"Better?"

"Yeah. This is harder than it looks." Her voice sounded distant, but it was there. She sat down in front of me as though she were expecting something. I smiled down at her and ran my fingers through her fur. She ducked her head low and arched her back to me. It wasn't until she started panting that I understood the importance of what she was going through. Her beast not only recognized its mate, but its alpha. I backed away and undressed. My shift took several minutes longer and was substantially more painful than Delaney's. With her beast's submission, mine needed to answer. I have never had the longing or real desire to be an alpha, until now. I felt like she was pulling something from me. Like she was asking a question that I alone could answer. I brought her out here to help her, but it seemed like she would be helping me as well.

Delaney was the most beautiful thing I'd ever seen as a human, and as a wolf she was just as majestic. As soon as my body finished its shift, I padded over to her. Again, she ducked her head. I opened my mouth and playfully bit her nose. Again, I tried to reestablish our connection. She was correct, it was a lot harder than I thought. When in my wolf form, it was easy to let go a bit of my control. To let the beast take over some, but for this kind of communication I had to reign the beast in, and that was incredibly difficult.

"Reid?" Delaney's soft voice rang in my mind. And like that, the connection snapped into place.

"I hear you."

She nipped my nose back in a chiding way and said, "See? Harder than it looks."

"I want to help you, but I need to see what you can do. I know you have hunted, can you call your lightning?"

"I think so. The only two times I hunted before, Mitch wouldn't let me try."

"Try now." I needed to see how different she was. I thought it would take her a few moments to call up her lightning, but in the blink of an eye she went nearly incandescent with lightning. She looked as though she was made from lightning. And her eyes sparked, looking as though they were their own lightning strikes. When she shook her fur out, sparks went flying off of her, reminding me of shooting stars. She was utterly stunning. I was captivated. Before I could say a word, she stalked toward me.

"Wait," I mentally called.

Her power was so strong that even from this distance I honestly didn't know if I could survive it. It wasn't just the lightning. Her lightning was part of it, but the magnitude of her power was pressing down on me and I wasn't sure even touching her would be a good idea.

She paused and in a tone that I couldn't recognize as her she said, "Reid, I'm scared. I can't pull my power back in."

She looked scared to death and her power was only growing. The force of her power was becoming increasingly more intense. It was causing the trees and brush to start bowing and giving way. I tried to hold my ground next to her, but her power was overwhelming.

"Love, you need to try …" I trailed off when I realized she wasn't just scared of her power, but about being a wolf. I had to bring her down. I could do this. She was my mate. I had to heal her. I *would* heal her.

DELANEY HAGEN

FOURTEEN

OH, GOD. MY heart was about to beat out of my chest. I was losing control. I couldn't even pull my lightning back into myself. I hated being in wolf form. I hated this side of myself and I was about to totally lose it. I couldn't catch my breath. I'd never pulled so much lightning out of my core before and was growing increasingly more worried I couldn't handle it. Not just the power, but this whole new life that was forced upon me. I could control nothing.

"Delaney." It was a distant voice. A calming one.

"Delaney, love." It was a voice breaking through the erratic thoughts. Even my vision began to clear.

The bright white and back began to fade into normal colors and hues.

"Reid, I can't do this. I need to change back," I pleaded. Even my mental voice was shaken.

"No. Delaney, you need to come to terms with this."

How? How can he ask that of me?

"You have no idea what this is like. You don't understand."

He could never understand.

"Don't I? Delaney, you were not the only one who lost everything when they were forcibly changed. I lost everything, Delaney. But, I gained so much more."

I felt my power slowly trickle back to my core. My heart rate began to slow with his words. I prayed he didn't truly understand.

"Tell me."

He did. He told me everything. He told me how he was attacked and changed. Then he told me about Beth. A woman who could never accept him or what he was.

"I would have denied this new part of myself to have her. I would have done anything. But she could never get past it."

Wasn't that what I was trying to do to myself? Deny this part of me? Ignore it was even there? All that I knew as a wolf was death and hunting. I seemed to only know pain and hurt.

We didn't speak for a long time. We just sat there in the middle of a small clearing surrounded by trees. Finally, my power returned to my core and I was left with the burning. There was so much burning. Everything seemed to burn.

"I don't know how to be okay with this."

"Then let me show you, love. Let me put you back together, because I need you whole to heal myself."

"Show me how to heal."

"Come, beautiful, let's run."

We ran. We didn't hunt or chase anything. I let my beast out and together we ran so far and fast I thought for just a moment that all of my self-loathing issues and problems were forgotten. Reid showed me that being a wolf and having this type of form was about freedom, not power. We ran for hours. We ran over downed trees and across small streams. The colors were brighter and scents were stronger. Reid showed me it could be fun to be a wolf. We played. Reid loved me and now he was showing me how to love my new self.

I looked up to the sky and realized it had moved substantially. It was getting late. I was about to ask him if he wanted to go, but his posture stiffened. He growled for a moment, then returned his attention to me. *What was that about?*

"Want to change and go back to Troy's?" he asked, as though nothing had happened.

"It's getting late, we should."

He padded up to me and licked my nose. Everything I'd experienced until this point had been all bad and none of the good. Reid was showing me that being a wolf and having this beast did not have to be so awful. He told me that he would put me back together, now I felt a piece of me click into place. I think he was right. He was putting me back together one damaged part at a time.

I shifted and went to find my clothes. Reid's shift took about five minutes and looked utterly painful.

The moment of the change for me has always been instant, but with Reid, it's a fight for control. His change seemed to be taking longer than normal. His mental change, that was. His physical form was him, but I could feel he wasn't settled. I finished slipping on my bra and my last pair of underwear then I walked over and went to place my hand on his cheek, but he caught my hand just before I could make contact. His eyes flickered from glowing green to caramel and back again. His grip was like steel and his gaze was a warning.

"Reid, you're hurting ... uff." I was cut off by the force at which I was shoved against the tree that stood directly behind me. My heart was beating wildly in my chest and I had to tamp down on the fear I was feeling. I knew from firsthand experience that fear would only make this situation worse. I was his mate. He couldn't hurt me. Right? He pinned both of my hands above my head and buried his face in the crook of my neck. He breathed in a deep inhale of my scent. I was trembling. Oh God, this was the same position I'd been in before with Mitch. Tears flooded my eyes, but they refused to fall. I tried to gulp air with hopes it would calm my wild thoughts. I began to hyperventilate anyway. Every time I tried to close my eyes, I saw Mitch's disgusting smile. I could scent my own fear despite my best effort to be calm.

I can't do this. I can't be the person I was before. I can't be the person he needs me to be.

I was having an internal struggle I couldn't seem to quell. It was such a feeling of duality. I was fighting the fearful and broken person I was and trying to be the strong and independent person I wanted to be.

His frenzy ebbed slightly. I'm sure he felt my panic through our connection. That word connection meant something. It was one of the many important things that separated Reid from Mitch. I had to push my fear aside. I had to be strong and move past this. Reid shifted his iron grip from my hands and he laced his fingers with mine. It was such an intimate gesture. I calmed appreciably. This was Reid. This way the man I would fight all of my inner demons for. And I would win.

Reid was fighting his own beast. I relaxed to his sensual onslaught. I was growing wet and knew by his deep growling he knew it. He shifted his big body so that he was pressed more firmly against me. I sucked in a breath, then I felt him hard against me. He moved my wrists to one of his huge hands. His other hand trailed down my side and settled on my hip. All the while, he never took his eyes off mine. His gaze no longer flickered from his steady caramel. They were his wolf's green.

"Reid, we need … oh goodness." My train of thought had been completely derailed by his hand slipping to my wet heat.

He didn't rip my panties off, he simply rubbed his thumb and finger along the drenched folds of my sex through them. I tried to stifle a whimper, but all of my control was slipping. With incredible speed Reid tore the scrap of cloth away and sank a finger deep inside of me. I cried out at the sudden intrusion. Oh God, it was more than welcome. He kept shaking his head as though he were trying to clear it.

"Mine," he growled next to my ear.

I tried to speak, but every time I tried to respond, his finger stirred inside me, causing my focus to break away completely. Finally, he slipped his finger from me. He then drew the wet coated digit to his mouth and sucked it. My jaw gaped, and my sex clenched in reaction. He dropped to his knees and threw one of my legs over his shoulder. I knew I should be stopping this. I knew when Reid finally did come back to himself he would … His tongue slipped between my folds and just like that my thoughts flew apart. He lapped at me with a hungry intensity that had me moaning. My hands slipped to his hair, and it took everything in me not to grab at him and pull him closer to me. His hands were pressed on my belly and thank God, because there was no way I could stand under his sensual assault.

His mouth settled until his lips covered my taut little bud. His eyes flicked up to mine. He sucked it in his mouth. I couldn't stop myself from screaming out and writhing against him. Building, the pressure was building, and this heat was nearing a fever pitch. I was only a few flicks of his wicked tongue from nearing my climax. I was thrusting to him with every pull. My body was aching for release. He slipped a finger inside of me as he flicked his tongue across my clit, and that was all it took. My world shattered, and my sex clenched around his finger, drawing him deeper. My fingers grasped his hair, drawing his face closer, and my vision blurred with the intensity of this orgasm. I was screaming and didn't even realize it until my throat grew raw. I looked down at Reid, who was not letting up one bit. Everything was getting too intense, and I tried to push him away; he snarled and nipped my inner thigh.

"Reid, please, I can't." My voice was a mere rasp. My voice seemed to jolt his awareness. He flew away from me. I all but crumpled to the ground, heaving for breath. I wasn't sure what just happened. I wasn't sure I was sorry it happened either. What exactly did he do to me? Lord help me, I wanted it to happen again.

"I'm sorry." His voice was guttural.

Wait, he was apologizing? Hell if I would let him feel bad about what he just did to me.

"I'm not."

His eyes flicked to me in question.

I gave him a shy smile and added, "You just devoured me." I was nearly breathless.

"My beast wouldn't go back in its cage without tasting you." He looked horrified.

I wanted to go to him, to reassure him that I loved him and that I was more than fine with what just happened. After being so devastated by him, my legs were little more than Jell-O.

"Reid, I'm sorry you had a struggle, but holy shit, man. There is nothing back there that I didn't enjoy." His features seemed to ease slightly with my words, so I didn't mention my own internal issues.

His eyes widened and rushed over to help me up. I couldn't help but giggle.

"Care to explain what exactly happened? Not that I'm complaining, mind you."

He set me on my feet and ran a hand through his tawny hair. In a low, controlled tone, he answered, "My beast needed you. I mean, I did too, and I think that's why the upper hand shifted. I mean we are one in the same, but it needed its mate."

I thought about how Reid was changed, and the events that followed made him hate this part of himself. He may be trying to help me gain some control of myself, but I think he needed to accept this part of himself as well.

"Reid, I'm not at all sorry for what happened. You shouldn't be either. This is part of who you are. I love you, wolf and all. I think it's time you love every part of yourself."

"Is it that obvious?"

For once, this male, my male, my alpha, wouldn't meet my eyes. If my heart weren't already his, it would have been. His expression was so defeated, and it nearly broke me.

"I know I'm not the authority on being what we are. But, Reid, hating yourself isn't helping your control. You're a lone wolf, I don't think that's what your beast wants. If you keep punishing yourself for what happened all those years ago, you'll never grow. I love every bit of you."

He seemed to be processing every word. Maybe he was looking for the lie in them. He wouldn't find it, because I truly believed every last word I spoke.

"I'll try, love." He kissed the tip of my nose. He then turned, saying, "We should dress and get back." He went to go dress, and I fumbled my way toward my clothes. I slipped my shirt on and then reached for my pants. I paused, looking for my underwear. I eyed the spot where Reid had, um, well, demolished me, and laying on the ground were what was left of my undergarment. I walked over and retrieved them. I held them up to inspect them.

"Reid?" I called.

"Yes?"

"Can we maybe take it easy on my underwear? This was my last pair." I slipped my pants on and just as I finished buttoning them I felt Reid's breath on my neck. I shivered in response. I couldn't help it. Damn him. He had a direct line to my hormones, and it bypassed everything else. *Lord, this man does things to me*.

"I like the idea of you wearing no panties."

His breath was warm on my neck, and it caused my pulse to flutter like the beating of a hummingbird's wing. My breaths grew shallow, and I couldn't seem to make a coherent thought.

"Um, shouldn't we ... I ... I mean we should ..." What was I saying? Oh God, his nearness was already effecting me. I was so easy when it came to Reid. He laughed low in his chest and then drew me to him. He covered my mouth with his. This wasn't a tentative kiss, this was one of possession and passion. He was kissing his mate, and he knew it. When he broke the kiss, I was heavy-lidded and breathless.

"Come, love, let's get back."

Words were a little more than I was currently capable of, so I nodded, and we walked to the car. Just as the car came into view, he paused and grabbed me, pushing me behind his body. I'd not expected this move, so I nearly tripped over my own feet trying to keep up with the movements.

"What the hell?" I asked the large back blocking my view. I heard him snarling.

Just what the hell is going on over there?

"Look, I know this looks bad, but I came here to talk."

I had no idea whose voice I was hearing, and it was pissing me off. The voice was male and young. Not teenage, but early twenties for sure. I put my hands on Reid's shoulders trying to see, but it was no use. I tried again to see over and around Reid. Just as I was about to jump to get a glance, Reid rushed the man. My weight had been on him, so the momentum sent me flying toward the ground. And, just like that, I got a face full of dust and dirt. I got a lovely mouthful of the gritty substance. I scrambled to my feet to see Reid holding someone against the car. Once I got to my feet, I walked slowly toward him. I scented the air, something I should have been doing this whole time. I tried to sift through the thirteen thousand different scents. My eyes went wide; it was a were. I swallowed. It wasn't Mitch, but this did not bode well.

I placed a hand on Reid's back, trying to calm him.

"Please, Mitch ... sent ... arg—" The man's words were being cut off by Reid's forearm that was crushing his windpipe.

"Reid, let him talk. Ease up, big guy. I'm okay. I'm here," I crooned to him, trying to coax him off the edge. After a few heartbeats, he eased off the man. His sand-brown hair matched his light-brown eyes. He stood a little taller than me, but shorter than Reid. My guess was five foot ten. He had a lean build. The man struck me as a surfer. Maybe it was the deep copper tan. He was cute in that, "yo dude," surfer kind of way. He couldn't have been more than twenty-two when he was changed. His eyes were darting around until they landed on me. His expression was so pained when he saw me he looked away quickly.

"You have only moments to explain before I let Reid have his way with you."

The man's hand flew to his red throat. He tried to speak a few times, but only coughing fits came out.

"Tyler. My name is Tyler."

Reid stiffened and dropped his head.

"Tyler, damn it, you looked different." Reid's tone was ashamed.

My eyes widened at him. Did he know him?

"It's okay, man. I can understand," Tyler gasped, while rubbing his neck.

"Explain, please." I was getting more than a little sick of not understanding.

"Mitch sent me here while he went north to find you. Now, he knows you're here. I'm to watch you and report back on your movements," he explained. Oh well, in that case ...

"So, why aren't we killing him?" I asked, looking to Reid.

"Good question." Reid took a step closer, and Tyler's hands flew up to gesture in a halting motion.

"Whoa, Reid wait. Let me explain."

Reid stopped.

"You know me, Reid. I need to explain everything. I helped Mitch break into the Coven. That's why he changed me. I'm an expert in nearly anything electronic. I thought at the time it wasn't a big deal, because, like most weres, I wanted to see the Coven destroyed."

He paused to gauge my reaction. I had none, as I was right there with him.

"Right after that, I left, because my job had me traveling to Saint Louis. When I got back, I heard of the murders. I swear I had no idea. Then everything with you happened."

He couldn't meet my eyes. He seemed ashamed. Good.

"None of this sat well with me. And the more I talked to others in the pack, the more they agreed."

My thoughts slid to Anderson and the phone call. Had he been telling the truth? When Tyler spoke, he was emotional, and I could feel the honesty in his words. Anderson? There was something that made me pause in believing him.

"Look, I know Anderson called you. He is one of Mitch's little bitches. There are a number of us who would fight with you. I have a plan—and I'll do what it takes to get you to trust me. All I ask is that you kill Mitch."

Reid and I exchanged a look. We both nodded and heard him out. It was the only thing we could do.

THE WHOLE AFTERNOON had started out pretty amazing; running and playing with Reid had eased me in some way. He calmed me. It was hard to explain just how he affected me, I just knew that he was my air. I needed him to breathe, for my heart to beat. Then the experience just after he changed had been intense, to say the least. Then there was Tyler. My gut told me trusting him was a good idea, but my history screamed to not trust anyone. The plan was pretty straightforward. It was all based on throwing Mitch off his center of balance.

The drive back had been uneventful, thank all that was holy. I had to talk Reid into stopping, so I could buy underwear. He may like the commando thing, but I, however, did not. I explained that he could rip them off like a present if he liked. He seemed to like that idea, so he bought me twenty pairs. That should last about a week.

When we pulled up to Troy's house, I heard Troy and Monique talking in the backyard. Okay, actually, I heard Troy bitching and Monique being exasperated. Yup, sounded about right. I bypassed the front door and went straight to the back of the house. The smell of smoke tickled my nose. It didn't seem like things with Troy's training were going well. Just as I entered the yard, I heard Tory's high-pitched, excited tone just as a tennis ball-sized fireball whizzed past my nose. I stood frozen for a moment, then turned to face Troy.

I narrowed my eyes and put my hands on my hips. "Christ man! Are you trying to kill me?"

His expression was sheepish when he squeaked, "Sorry, it just slipped out."

"That's what she said!" I heard Garrett's voice call from the porch.

Okay, I couldn't help it. I busted out with laughter. I had to nearly hold my stomach from laughing so hard. Troy was nearly beside himself. Finally, after a few minutes, we were both calmed.

"I see training is going well." I flicked my gaze to Monique, who looked less than amused.

"He has so much power it's a little scary, but he can't control it. Fire is such a fickle power. I'm trying though." She honestly sounded defeated.

"How about I tag in and give you a break?"

She smiled and nodded.

I turned to Troy and narrowed my eyes. "Okay, hooker, show me what you can do."

In response, he lifted up his hands and called his power to him. His palms glowed orange before two small flames appeared and flickered before going out. He, much like Monique, looked defeated. My heart ached for him, it also settled my resolve. I had to help him. I just had to break through his thick skull.

I walked to Garrett and leaned close to his ear and whispered, "I swear, no matter what, I won't hurt you. Trust me." I leaned up. He had a confused look on his face. I got up and walked to Troy.

"Come here, Troy. We need to talk," I called to him, motioning toward me. He hesitated, but listened.

"Garrett, can you stand up?" I called to the tall man lounging on the porch. Troy would seriously hate me for what I was about to do, but it may be the only way to get him to focus on this. Garrett stood and took a few steps closer. I held up my hand for him to stop, and he did. I left my hand outstretched toward him and turned my face to Troy.

"You stand right there." I pointed to a spot just to my left. So Troy was only a few feet away on one side and Garrett stood several yards to my right, on the stairs leading up to the porch. I took a deep breath. *Please don't hate me for this*. I pulled my lightning from my core to my outstretched right hand. Troy's expression was confused.

Without taking my eyes off Troy, I said, "Garrett, don't move no matter what, do you understand me?"

Troy's eyes went wide with incredulity as Garrett replied, "Uh, okay." I winked at him, and he nodded.

I pulled harder on my power, causing pops and arcs of electricity in my palm. It set my nerve endings alight. I had a lot more control of my ability than Troy did, but that did not make me perfect. Right now, I had to be.

"Delaney, don't play like this," Troy warned, taking a step forward. As he did, I did as well. He paused, seeing I was very serious.

I flicked a finger, sending a small jolt to land about five inches in front of Garrett's feet. Troy was getting pissed. I walked a little closer to Garrett. I flicked another small ball of lightning. Garrett jumped, but didn't move.

"Stop me, Troy." I now stood in the middle of the two men, both of whom looked utterly terrified.

"Delaney, this isn't funny."

I flicked again. Troy jumped. I took another step toward Garrett.

"I know that better than anyone. I have lost nearly everyone. I refuse to lose you because you can't get your head out of your ass."

We had no time to ease him into this power. He didn't need to be perfect, he had to try though.

I took two steps this time and sent a larger ball of lightning to the ground about three inches from Garrett's left shoe.

Garrett's eyes were pleading with Troy to try. Garrett knew just how important this was.

That look seemed to do something to Troy. His hands began to glow. He was ready to try. I flicked another bolt this time, hitting so close to Garrett it sent shivers through the large man. Troy's hands went up in reflex and a small fireball went wild.

I took a deep breath. I was one good leap to getting to Garrett. I turned to face Troy and pulled yet more power. The lightning was now climbing up my arms. The air grew heavy with the scent of ozone.

"Last chance, Troy." I knew I would pull my power in at the last moment, but I thought Troy doubted it. Especially after he witnessed my lack of control in my wolf form. I knew he could do this. I needed him to know it now.

I turned and leapt for Garrett. I heard both men scream right before I was slammed directly in the chest with a bowling ball-sized fireball. Thank God, at the last moment I shifted my hands and my power took the brunt of his attack. The force of his power sent me flying off into the brush of Troy's yard. My hands burned and the heat from the blast nearly singed my eyebrows. I lay in the yard a little dazed. I blinked rapidly and pulled the rest of my power to my core. I still smelled smoke, and the heat was getting unbearable. I looked down to realize my shirt was on fire. I rolled in the grass. Note to self: Stop, drop and roll ain't no joke. Had he wanted to hurt me, no stop, drop and roll would have worked, not with magical fire. The small flames were extinguished in short order with my flailing. It took me a few moments to get up, but I did manage it. The amount of power that took was astounding. I had no idea if Troy really knew what he had done.

I looked at Troy, who was hugging Garrett. It honestly made me happy that he found him. Then Troy released the bigger man and he stalked toward me. I braced myself. He was livid, and it radiated off him in heat waves. He had every right to be. I should have found a better way …

His arms wrapped around me in a hug. I stood there a little dumbfounded. I'd expected to be yelled at, slapped or even punched. Hell, I'd seen Troy dump so many drinks on people I half expected him to go into the house and pour one to dump over my head. But no, he was hugging me. I hugged him back.

"You're so lucky I figured out how to do that or I would have had to kill you."

"Nah, I pulled my power in. Thank God I had enough to take the full force of your power, because, Troy, that was a major power. And I swear Garrett knew I would never hurt him." I glanced to the tall man and he nodded. Thank God he wasn't a cash register, because if he were, his ass would be a melted heap of disaster.

"It just clicked. I think it was the fact that you have lost so much and here you were worrying about me."

"Is he mad?" I wasn't sure I wanted to know the answer.

He shook his head in negation and replied, "He saw you drawing your power in, and he said he trusted you. Me, I wasn't sure, honestly. Please never do that again."

We separated and Troy looked utterly pleased with himself.

"I'm badass."

"Yeah, Troy, you're pretty badass. But I would still keep an extinguisher nearby."

He was about to give me some pithy retort I was sure, but his words were cut off by Monique's bright tone.

"Delaney! You have a package."

I froze.

Who the hell could be sending me anything? Troy's head tilted in confusion at me. I shrugged.

"You been doing some online shopping?" he questioned.

Monique trotted in the backyard carrying a large brown box with FedEx overnight stickers plastered all over it. She set it on the small table and I walked over. Reid soon appeared in the doorway of the house. My eyes flicked to him. He smiled, then frowned.

"Been doing laundry again?" His voice seemed to always warm my skin even from a distance. I smiled and detoured to him.

"No. Why ask?"

"Your shirt now matches several I have seen before." His eyes went to my chest.

I looked down to see a number of small holes dotting my once whole shirt. Great. I stopped just in front of him and gave him a quick kiss. He inhaled a deep breath as I leaned in. He froze. He went completely rigid. Had I forgotten deodorant? I lifted my arm and sniffed. No, I was good.

"What?"

"I smell blood. Are you cut or burned?" His tone sounded as though he knew the answer but didn't want to admit it. I shook my head. His eyes were locked on the box. My heart stopped and dropped to my feet. Slowly, I walked toward it. I breathed deep and then I caught the scent as well. The air was thick with the metallic tang that was blood. My mouth watered in response. I hated that it had that effect on me, but this wasn't the time for self-loathing. I stood in front of the box but couldn't make myself open it. We all stood around this package as though we were waiting for it to jump up and open itself. I didn't dare move. Maybe if no one moved, or did anything, we wouldn't have to admit what was in that box.

Garrett shifted and I heard the click of a knife. He reached for the box and ran the blade along the seam of tape that sealed it. I swallowed the impossibly large lump that formed in my throat. I reached out and lifted up the flaps. There was a small white Styrofoam cooler with crumpled brown paper sounding it. Sitting just on top was a small white envelope with my name penned on it. I picked it up and slipped a shaking finger under the sealed edges. I pulled a small white card out. I spared a glance down at my chest. I could visibly see my heart beating, hammering my chest wall so hard. I took a deep breath and opened it.

Delaney,

This is a token of my love for you. Please enjoy this gift. See you soon.

Love,

Mitch

I grew cold and dropped the note. I couldn't make myself open the cooler. I began shaking. Fear. He would find me. He would take me and do things to me. Force me to … I felt Reid's arm snake around my waist. He pulled me to his chest.

"Shh, love, you aren't helpless. You have us, and you have a lot of power."

He reached for the note and picked it up. He scanned it and handed it to Monique. She did the same until everyone had read it.

"There's no going back for any of us," Monique intoned, looking at the box.

"Shit just got real. But I have no fucks to give." Troy's gaze was locked on the cooler.

Garrett's words were laced with disappointment. "As much as I want to help I think I'm better off here. You know, human and all." He was right. "But I would if I could," he added. His eyes met mine; I couldn't hold his gaze for long. I never wanted to bring this to any of them. I glanced back at him, trying my best not to seem so crestfallen over this whole debacle.

I gave him a shy smile. I nearly fell in love with him in that moment for his genuine willingness to help.

Then, like a wave crashing into me, I was wracked with guilt. All of these people were putting their lives on the line, and I had no right to ask them to. What if they met the same fate as Sierra and Mil? I would break if something happened to any of them. I felt

Reid's breath on my ear, and that seemed to calm my thoughts slightly.

"We want to be here. We want to do this. Calm down, love." His words acted as a soothing balm to my wild emotions. I took in a deep breath and held it. After a few moments, I let it out. I needed to just do this. Rip the damn Band-Aid off.

I reached for the lid.

"Wait!" Troy nearly screamed.

I jumped and almost peed my pants.

"Good lord, Troy! What?" I asked, covering my heart with my right hand. The man had nearly given me a heart attack.

"What are the chances it's steak? You know, like one of those Omaha steaks of the month club things?"

We all just blinked at him. *Steak of the month club? Really?*

I tried to speak, but words failed me. I just shook my head at him. Then, reluctantly, I reached for the box and tentatively lifted the lid. I dropped it to the table, and we all leaned in to peer into the cooler.

We all stood staring at the object that lay within. My hand flew to my mouth to stifle a scream.

"Oh, hell naw!" Troy yelled, running for the tree line.

I heard his muffled heaves and wretches off in the distance.

"Who?" Monique questioned, never taking her eyes off the gruesome sight.

Tucked neatly in the cooler were two human hands. One hand was male, and the other looked to be female. They were interlaced as though they were holding on for dear life. The female had had an engagement ring and wedding band still snugly in place. Both hands looked to have been ripped off. Wait, no, not ripped. Bitten off.

"It's Mark and I'm assuming that's his wife," I intoned, unable to take my eyes from the contents of the box. I had to blink rapidly to clear the buildup of unshed tears. More people who had been hurt because of me. Reid was talking to me, trying to pull my attention from the hands. His words fell away before I could hear them. Then it hit me. This wasn't my fault. This was Mitch. This was all his doing. I narrowed my eyes and for first time in the past six months, I knew what I needed to do. I felt strong, I felt unstoppable.

Mitch had sent this to frighten me. He wanted to put a nail in my coffin. The reality was that he sent me the fuel I needed to do everything in my power to kill him. Fuck him being my maker. I would do what I had to. I heard a sharp crack of lightning not too far in the distance and knew that my power was building. Mitch had no idea just what was coming for him. He was going to have one hell of a storm on his hands, because I was so very done being weak.

I was so much like the power I could control. It was time to become the lightning.

DELANEY HAGEN
FiFTEEN

"MIST AGAIN?" I asked as I ran my hand through the dense fog. I watched as it swirled and danced around my fingers. I was again in a field surrounded by birch trees, but strangely it smelled of juniper berries. I inhaled the scent. I knew where I was. But I had no idea if he would be here. The man who had plagued my dreams since I was a child. The same man who had all but abandoned me for the past few months.

"I like it. It's mysterious."

He would say that. He had jokes, and I had fog. His voice seemed to bounce off the trees, shaking them slightly. I whirled around, still unable to see him. But I felt him.

"Was that a joke? Did you get a sense of humor while you were away?" I knew my hackles were up, I couldn't help it.

"Maybe."

I rolled my eyes. Why couldn't he be direct?

After a few moments, he appeared. Well, maybe solidified is a better word. The mist seemed to coalesce into his shape and he slowly stepped from it.

"That's a neat trick."

"Shall I show you how to do it?"

My eyebrows raised in excitement. Could he really do that? Then I narrowed my gaze at him. "You won't. So, why offer?"

His laugh filled the field and sent lightning to spark over my whole body. I shivered at the sensation. God, but his laughter made me want to bathe in it. It was almost as though he set every nerve ending on fire. Like he pulled my lightning from me and made it dance on the surface of my skin.

"Who are you?" It was a whisper. I didn't think he would answer, but when he did, I was in shock.

"I'm a god of old. But if I told you I was a father to you, you wouldn't believe me."

Much like his laughter had, his words caused my lightning to stir. I shuddered.

Um, I had a father. Not too sure what he was getting at.

"I don't understand."

"Oh, lightning bug, I am the father of your power. You are just as much mine as your human parents. Part of me lives in you."

My heartbeat picked up. His words sounded so true that I wanted to believe them. How though? Wait, he was a god?

"So, you're a god and I'm what? Like your daughter?"

He waved the question away, clearly done with the interrogation. He walked over to me. He was a large man. Not as big as Reid, but just as tall. He reached out and, with light fingers, lifted my hand and turned it up so the palm was facing him. He gave me a knowing smirk as he glanced at the bite mark. Heat flushed my cheeks. Men, god or not, were all the same. I would be willing to bet that he was mentally giving

Reid a high five. Then I felt him. He was pulling lightning from me. Pulling the power from my core. I nearly staggered back in shock.

"See, bug, it is of me and mine to control."

It was so raw. He was stripping the power from me in such a way that felt like an invasion. I wanted to scream at him to stop. It felt like he was ripping my soul out of my body. I opened my mouth to beg him to stop, but in the next moment it was back, and he simply stood there stroking a finger over the red scar on my wrist. I was panting, trying to take gulps of air, and there was Captain freaking America standing tall and so smug. I tried not to roll my eyes at him, really I did.

"Okay, if you're a god and you have this paternal connection to me …" I met his eyes, wanting him to feel my next words, "Then why?" I felt no need to go any further with my questioning. He knew the why I was referring to. Why leave me? Why have me experience so damned much pain and loss? Why not stop Mitch from breaking me?

"Oh, lightning bug, sometimes the most beautiful of flowers and the strongest of trees are that way because they had to fight to grow." His tone was final, and I knew I would get no more, much less an apology from him. So damned cryptic. Why couldn't he be straightforward? I bet he got off on this crap. He probably sat in his man cave laughing at the rest of us.

"How can I kill Mitch?" It was a simple question, but I honestly didn't think he would answer.

"Delaney, what are you?"

"I don't understand." I quirked an eyebrow at him and he narrowed his dark eyes.

"When you think of what you are, what you have become. What are you?"

The truth? I had no idea.

Before my change I would have said witch, but now I really didn't know. He must have seen the discomfort of his question on my face because he walked over and placed a hand under my chin, pulling my gaze to his.

"You need to figure out what you are. When you do, you'll be able to kill Mitch."

Had he been any other man standing this close to me, it would feel awkward, but his touch brought only comfort. Had he been a blanket I would have covered myself with him. And that kind of pissed me off. What was I? I wasn't a witch, not anymore. I wasn't a werewolf. I didn't have a painful transition and I retained all of my power.

Could I be something new?

"Bug, the Coven must be taken care of. They are polluting our people."

"How?"

He smiled. He released his hold on my chin and backed away. I knew he wouldn't answer. Hey, can't blame a girl for trying.

"Remember, Delaney, you never did follow the rules. Why would now be any different?"

I had no idea what he meant, but I guess I would have to figure it out.

"Oh, one more thing. You have a letter to read, don't you?"

His voice got to me after his body dissipated into the mist. Damn, the letter from Mil! I'd forgotten, again. I walked the few steps to where he had disappeared. There was a small gold coin laying in the spot he had just been. I picked it up. There was a spoked wheel on one side and a lightning bolt on the other.

"Cryptic god!" I yelled to nothing. Just before I woke up though, I swore I felt his warm laughter surround me.

I didn't wake up in a rush. It was as though I was eased into wakefulness. I lay there trying to understand everything I'd learned. Most of it had been this read-between-the-lines bullshit. I flexed my hand and felt the cool metal of the coin resting in it. I shoved the small gold disk under my pillow. I needed to make a mental checklist of stuff I needed to do.

One: Figure out what I was.

Two: Kill Mitch.

Three: Take down the Coven.

Four: Get a brownie.

Five: Live happily ever after.

The last two might have been stretching it. I was forgetting something though, or at least I thought I was. Who was I kidding? If, and that was a huge if, I could kill Mitch, how the freaking holy hot sauce would I bring down the Coven? I groaned and rolled to my side. Reid's caramel gaze met mine.

"Bad dream?" His voice was rough. He must have just awoken as well.

"Something like that. What time is it?"

"Nearly nine. We should probably get up. We don't have a lot of time before Mitch will come and I have a small idea of how to deal with him."

I raised an eyebrow at him hoping he would continue, but he just smiled and kissed me.

It was a light kiss that I quickly deepened into something more. He pulled back. I whined in protest. Damn him.

"I know what you're doing. You're trying to distract me so we can forget about everything." His tone was chiding. He was right, well partly. I wanted to distract myself.

The damn letter! He must have been leaning in for another kiss when I jumped out of the bed. He face planted right where I was sitting. I ran around the room looking for clothes.

Shit, wait, where is my purse? I don't need clothes!

"You know, if you didn't want to kiss me you could have told me."

His tone was joking, but I had to find that purse.

Where the hell had I put the damn thing?

I knew I looked like a crazy person but I had to ... the bathroom!

I ran to the small room and there was my small purse hanging on a hook just on the other side of the door. I unzipped it and reached in, feeling the letter immediately. My stupid hands were shaking. Two times now the person in my dreams had reminded me. It was time to figure out what the damn thing said. Maybe it would clue me in to just what I was. I slowly walked over to the bed and placed the letter on it. Never taking my eyes off it, I tossed on a shirt and shorts.

"Is that the letter Mil wrote you?" Reid asked.

I nodded, then sat on the bed and picked the letter up. The wax seal had been broken from the last attempt at reading it. I fingered my name. My heart was stabbed with loss at seeing Mil's handwriting. I could do this.

The parchment was thick. It was the kind that Mil loved. *When you write a letter, the paper you use tells a lot about you*, Mil always said. I pulled the letter out and unfolded it.

Delaney,

I owe you more than a mere letter, but you need to know I did not tell you everything. I thought that I would have more time. It would seem as though my time is up. First, know how much I love you and keeping this prophecy from you was something I felt, at the time, was in your best interest. Here is the prophecy in its entirety: It was said that a Witch of new would have the power of the storm. She would willingly lay down her life to the spirit of the wolf and become that of old. She would be the final sacrifice. She will bring the corrupt down and cement her place at the head of her people. When she is mated she will start the line of old over again. She is the beginning of the old and the ending of the new.

This is the prophecy, my darling girl. I wanted to stop it from happening. I wanted to prevent you from experiencing any pain. But I cannot. Just know that when I am gone, I will be with you always. And tell Troy he is welcome for the gift I will be giving him.

I love you daughter mine,
Mil

What. The. Actual. Hell. Did that even mean? I handed the letter to Reid. I understood all of the prophecy. All but one line. The bit about me being mated. Did that mean what I thought it meant? No. No. It couldn't.

I looked to Reid, whose eyes went wide. Oh yeah, I was betting he just got to that part.

"Well, that wasn't straightforward or anything," he finally commented in a sarcastic tone.

"Yeah." It was all I could say. *Oh shit.* We both sat on the bed not talking, not voicing our thoughts. I thought I would be in tears, but I was in too much shock for that.

"So, that part about being mated. Does it mean what I think it means?" Reid finally asked.

All I did was nod. I mean what else could I do? This letter basically just said that all the things that should be impossible weren't.

Surprise! Not only can you be turned into a werewolf, you can get pregnant too.

"Okay." He was a little dazed, but he seemed calm. Calm? I was having a panic attack of epic proportions over here and mister big bad was calm.

"I think I can kill Mitch," I intoned, not meeting his eyes.

"Delaney, you can't kill your maker. It's impo …" I held up a hand, stopping him.

"I'm not a werewolf. I'm not bound by those laws or compulsions. Come on, I think I know what I am. Let's go find Monique. I want to be sure."

REiD JAMiSON

SiXTEEN

WELL THAT LETTER was ... enlightening.
And Delaney looked freaked out, to say the least. I
wondered which part freaked her out the most. My
fear was with this news, she would draw away from
me. We had been through hell and back and I wouldn't
let her run from me. After the shock of the contents of
that box, she could have crumbled. Damn if she looked
more pissed off and seemed to have this drive about
her. I was so proud of her. Now, this letter, the
knowledge that her future had been mapped out for
her, seemed to really scare the shit out of her. Or was it
that we could have children? I mean, did she not want
children or did she not want them with me? I'd given

up hope of that long ago, but now that it was possible, my heart began to swell with just the thought of it. Delaney didn't need more on her plate. She needed to be supported. I needed to put my own personal feelings and thoughts aside.

When she got up from the bed and finished getting ready for the day, she seemed almost somber. I wanted to know what she was feeling, but knew she needed to be sure about the prophecy before she would put words to her feelings. It just hurt my heart that I couldn't offer her solace.

Finding Monique had been easy, as she and Troy were working in the backyard.

"Monique, do you have a moment?" I called from the porch.

She looked up and nodded. She walked toward me with a small smile on her face.

"Hello, Reid. What's up?"

I handed her the letter. Delaney needed to be alone for a few moments, and I wanted Monique to be ready for the conversation. As she read, her face gradually fell. When she finished, her mouth was set in a white line.

"Listen, we have been told half-truths this whole time. Delaney and I need to know everything. We need to know about the past and the prophecy. We need to know it all. You're the only one who can tell us."

I met her dark eyes. She needed to know just how firm I was on this. So, I added the one thing I knew would break any doubt or loyalty she had to the Coven.

"You owe it to her."

Her head dropped in resignation. She nodded, not meeting my eyes. What could she have said? The whole fucking Coven owed her. I owed her. We both walked into the living room and waited on Delaney to come in. Knowing Delaney, she was trying to avoid it. If it were up to her, we would be waiting here for another few hours. As much as I didn't want to rush her, time was not on our side. We wouldn't wait for Mitch to come here, we would go to him. We needed to take him unaware.

It only took Delaney twenty minutes. She looked so defeated. My heart ached for her. She sat down next to me with her feet tucked up under her. She looked like she was trying to make herself a smaller target. As though whatever was to come wouldn't hit her. It was hard enough seeing her pain, but now, with our connection, I could feel it. I grabbed her hand and laced our fingers together. She was mine, and I protect what's mine.

"Is it all true? Is that all of it?" she asked.

Monique seemed uncomfortable, but resigned.

"Yes. Please know it's ingrained in us when we enter the inner circle that this prophecy is to be kept hidden."

"I want to know about our origins. Mil told me, but I want to hear it from you. I want to be sure about everything."

"Werewolves and witches came from one being. Druids." With the mention of Druids, Delaney seemed to breathe again. Even a small amount of tension left her body.

"When the Druids stopped the human sacrifices, the power split. Originally, we had the power to shift into an animal and control any earthly ability. When the powers split, the witches' powers were greatly diminished. And the werewolves kept the strength, but lost the magic. They tried to change witches at first, hoping that would unite the power again, but it didn't work. Well, not until you."

"Why hide this? If they wanted the powers brought back together, why not just be open about it. Hell, why wouldn't they want me to be turned?" I'd been wondering this same question.

"The Coven has changed. They have become self-serving and power hungry. They have been looking for you for years. They knew Mil had something to do with it, but no one could find her."

"Why did they want me?"

"They wanted to use your power and then they would breed you. They knew all of your offspring would be what we used to be."

"So, I can have children?"

My heart was racing with that question.

"Yes, but only with a mate. I don't know how that works. As witches, we love like humans. Werewolves are a little different in that regard." Her eyes flicked from me to Delaney and back. I was sure she knew.

An uncountable amount of heartbeats had gone by before she spoke again, "What am I?"

Monique seemed troubled by the question. She shifted and seemed to be giving the question serious consideration.

"Delaney, I think you are as we used to be, and if I had to put a name to it, I would say you're a Druid."

Why did that word, Druid, seem to carry so much weight? I looked over to Delaney. This news had shocked me. I thought she was a werewolf like me now. I should have known better. My Delaney was different. She was perfect. I just hoped she could see what I always had. When I met her eyes, she didn't look shocked. Instead, she had a wicked smile on her face. A knowing smile. I raised an eyebrow at her in question.

"I don't have to follow the rules you're bound by. I was born to break them."

She was staking her claim. She was stalking her kill. Druid, witch, it didn't matter, she was all wolf, all predator. I couldn't be prouder of my mate, my Delaney.

"Reid, you said you had a plan. I need to hear it."

Her tone was icy, and I almost felt bad for Mitch. Okay, not at all did I feel bad for him. I just hoped when it came down to it, my wolf would let her have the kill.

"Well, this whole thing with Anderson, as we know, was a ploy. Simply to make us wait for Mitch to amass power and come here."

"I agree, when I heard about it, it sounded like some mind trick Mitch would play," Monique added.

"Well, what do you think we should do?" Delaney asked.

"I think we need to ambush him. Hit him hard and fast. Power or not, we can't wait until the full moon. I have a plan, but it will take you, Monique, and Troy. Especially Troy. This all hinges on his ability. And one other person."

After I detailed my plan, everyone looked cautious. Hell, I had no idea if this would even work. Delaney had been through so damned much that it had to work. It just had to.

"I'll go tell Troy," Delaney stated as she got up and walked out the back door.

I immediately felt the loss of her. Touching her, hell, just being near her, felt so damned right. After the months of not having her around me, I had to fight the urge to go after her. And oh the things I'd done to her and still wanted to do to her.

"So, she's your mate then?" Monique's voice seemed to jolt me from my thoughts.

I nodded. I couldn't place Monique's expression. It seemed odd to me. And that sparked my curiosity.

"Well, let's hope she's not expecting. That would sure make this more difficult."

It would, but why did something seem wrong about her tone?

"Did you tell us everything about the prophecy?"

Her eyes widened at the question.

"Yes, Reid, I did. I know you don't trust the Coven as a whole, and the inner circle did nothing to help you, but I swear I have told you everything."

I believed her when she said she told us everything, but still there was something. I think I was over thinking the situation. Monique had proven helpful and was willing to lay down everything and fight Mitch. That alone spoke volumes. I nodded and then got up and walked to the back door. Troy sat behind Delaney doing something to her hair. Every time he lifted a brown lock up and twisted it, it seemed to spark with red firelight. She looked happy. Her eyes flicked to me, and they sparked with silver then returned to their gray. I growled in response. I couldn't help it. She must have heard me, because a bright smile spread across her face.

"D, your hair's a mess. I refuse to be seen out in public with you until something is done with it. So stop moving. Don't worry, I got this," Troy assured her.

"You know, Troy, nothing scares me more than you saying you got this. Talk about the fear of God."

He pulled her hair and she shouted in pain, then they both started laughing. Something I wasn't sure I would ever hear again. This whole thing had changed the woman I loved. It had hardened her to the world. It had opened her eyes to everything. In that moment, she was my Delaney, my sweet mate. She was strong and could protect herself. Not all bad came out of this.

The words from my dream so long ago came back to me in a rush. "Reid, she is breaking." The words had nearly killed me. It seemed like she had to break. And now she was who she was always meant to be … Mine.

She tentatively reached up to touch the mess atop her head. Her eyes went wide, and she turned to face Troy.

"It's worse than when you started!"

"I'm a drag queen, not a miracle worker!" Troy exclaimed, eyeing the mess that was her hair. "I can't be in public with you like this, go shower and then we will go."

Go? My hackles rose at the thought of her going off in the city alone. Okay, not that Savannah was a big city, I just didn't like the idea. Delaney stiffened and looked over at me. She could tell I didn't much like the thought.

"Delaney." I tried to keep the warning out of my voice, I failed utterly.

"Reid," she said as she walked over and stood just a few inches from me.

Her scent assailed my nose. That scent of gardenias and ozone spiked with the faintest spice of her arousal. It made my chest tighten and things began to stir in me. She had me wrapped around her finger. I was beginning to think she knew it. This little female could bring me to my knees, and there would be little I could do about it.

"We are going to pick up a few things and stop off at a favorite spot to train."

There was no question.

She used her two fingers to walk up my chest. Each small digit left a heated trail that went straight to my shaft. It wasn't until her pinkie finger slipped between buttons of my shirt that I realized I'd stopped breathing. She was playing me, and there was nothing I could do. I swallowed the large lump that was tightly situated in my throat. It did little to elevate the building pressure in my body. I wrapped my arms around her waist and pulled her to me, burying my face in the crook of her neck and inhaling. She gasped. I looked past her to Troy.

"She will be ready in an hour and a half." My tone was guttural. Without another word, I turned and walked her to our bedroom. I needed her and only right now would do. Right now, with my Delaney.

DELANEY HAGEN

SEVENTEEN

TRUE TO REID'S word, I was out of the house with Troy in an hour and a half. I knew it was a dirty tactic to use sex against him, but I needed to get away for a time. Though I don't in any way, shape or form feel bad about what had transpired between us. God, our chemistry was combustible. Every time we were alone, the fumes of our desire only seemed to build. It would only take one tiny spark to ignite it and then, boom went the goddamned dynamite and we would be completely engulfed. I loved him and the passion we shared. In a perfect world, we would be together for all time.

However, my world was anything but perfect. I was about to do something that he would grow to hate me for. I didn't think I could live with myself if something happened to Troy or Monique, but I would refuse live with myself if something happened to Reid. I shook my head to try to loosen the doubt that was creeping in. I had to be absolutely resolute in this. I was protecting him. I was protecting all of them. I would go to Mitch and kill him myself. He had no idea I could kill him. Hell, I didn't think I could. There had always been some force stopping me. *I wonder if it had been me stopping myself the whole time.*

"I know you did not drag me out here to go buy clothes. What's going on in that head of yours, Delaney?" Troy asked, never taking his eyes off the road.

I sighed. He knew me too well.

"Troy, I just need more shorts. Reid keeps ripping them off of me. It's either that or I'm going to have to walk around bottomless all day."

He looked aghast and sped up, "Ew, don't nobody want to see that!"

Gee, thanks. He had no idea I was going to ditch him and head north. I was such a shit friend. The thought of Troy dead because of a choice I made caused my throat to tighten and my stomach to lurch painfully. I looked at his thin face. The fine bones were so feminine and nearing on delicate. He was anything but. I couldn't live with it. I just couldn't. So much had changed in the last few months. I died, was changed, then I changed. I know the last two things sounded the same, but they weren't. I was forced to change both into something physically and mentally different. I could have crumbled or adapted. I had to fight to get to Reid, and that's what I did. I chose to change and became what was needed. And now I would do what was needed again. I would protect my mate and my friends.

"Okay, fine, but can we class it up and go to Target? I don't think my heart can take seeing the people of Walmart right now."

"That's fine. Oh, by the way, Mil left me a letter before she died and in it she wanted me to tell you …" I cleared my throat and in my best Irish accent said, "You're welcome."

He very nearly swerved off the Truman.

"Holy shit, man!"

"Girl, you have a real problem dropping bombs on me while I'm driving, don't you?"

"Sorry, I guess I didn't think it was a bomb."

"That old hooker knew!" His knuckles went white on the steering wheel.

We both fell silent until he pulled into the Target parking lot.

"I loved her, you know. It's just like the old bat to get the last word in," Troy finally spoke.

"I know, and she loved you."

OKAY, I'M GOING to throw a ball of lightning at you and I want you to block it. Don't worry if you miss, it will only knock you out, not kill you." I hoped. Months ago, I would have never assured him of this. Since my change and accepting just what I was, it all seemed to click.

"Great … I'm feeling really confident about this whole idea," he yelled back sarcastically.

I couldn't say I blamed him. A bead of sweat rolled down my back and pooled at the base of my spine. I was nervous. I felt deep in my bones that I had full control now. That I was what I was always meant to be. I could do this and doubt would only hinder me. I pulled a small pulse of power from my core and focused it in my hand. I glanced up at Troy, who looked nervous. I threw it at him.

He threw his hands up and dove to the ground. I shook my head and called to him, "Well, that's one way to dodge it."

"Sorry, I panicked."

He got up and dusted himself off. He then reached for his hair and smoothed it down. He narrowed his eyes at me and called, "I swear to dear sweet little baby Jesus, you mess my hair up, and I'll break you like a twig!"

I rolled my eyes, a gesture I knew he couldn't see.

"You going to keep bitching or do you want to pull up your big girl panties and do this?" I called to him.

He put his hands on his hips and jutted a foot out. "If we are talking about your panties, then yes they really are big."

He did not just say that! I pulled from my core and flung a small ball of lightning careening toward his head. He threw his hands up and screamed like a banshee. My ears were nearly ringing after that high-pitched wail. I think he hit a note that it would take most men a swift kick in the balls to achieve. He pulled on his core at the same time and deflected the ball of lightning with his fire.

"See, I told you you could do it!" I said, running toward him. He threw up his hands and the bastard sent a fireball hurtling toward me. I deflected it easily.

"What the hell?" I asked breathlessly.

"That's what you get! Okay, it may have been an accident, but nothing more than you deserve."

I shrugged. I could accept that.

"Delaney, what are you planning?"

I froze. There was no way he knew I was planning anything.

"Planning?" I scoffed nonchalantly.

He narrowed his eyes at me and didn't say a word. He did this thing where he looked at me and just waited. It reminded me of when I would be in trouble with Mil. Normally, I would break out into sobs and confess everything. I bit my lower lip to keep from doing just that.

"I want to face Mitch alone." As soon as the words fell out of my mouth, I wanted to stuff them right back in. I didn't want to hurt him by lying to him.

Just what you are doing to Reid. Shut up, self!

"Oh, is that all?"

My mouth hung open in shock. "Uh …" Was all I could manage.

"Girl, I knew you would want to do some shit like that."

"Uh, you did?" How could he possibly?

I heard a car pull up, and I whirled to face it. It was Monique and Reid. He looked pissed, even from this distance. I felt like a kid who had been caught with a hand in the cookie jar. *Shit.*

"You didn't have to call them," I muttered to Troy.

"Yes, I did! You would have hit me with a lightning ball, knocked me out and taken my keys," he offered with complete confidence.

"Ah, I wouldn't have done anything like that!" Yes, that's exactly what I planned. Holy hot sauce, Batman, was I that easy to read? I needed to make a mental note to myself that on my list of possible careers, nefarious mastermind was not one of them.

The passenger side car door swung open and the fumes spilling off Reid hit me before he even got out of the vehicle. *Well, shit.* Was this really that bad of an idea? I thought back. Going in alone to face Mitch and whoever was currently with him.

On a scale of Einstein to this year's Darwin Award winner, I thought this would fall at about a negative sixteen. I could hear Darwin weeping for me. I could kick myself. I didn't even need Reid to come lay into me. I got it just by the expression on his face.

Every step that brought him closer made it easier to see the anguish and pain on his face. *Oh, crap, way to F this up, Delaney.* I just wanted to keep everyone safe. I couldn't meet his eyes.

"I just wanted to fight this fight alone. I wanted to keep everyone safe."

My voice was small, because the excuse fell flat on my lips.

"Delaney, you thought going in against nearly ten, or more, adult male werewolves was a good idea?"

Well, when you put it like that ... I didn't respond to Reid's' question.

"Girl, I don't know what you're smoking, but sister you been holdin' out and clearly it's some good shit."

Reid put his hand against my cheek and raised my head to look at him.

"Love, I know you want us safe. But let us help you."

He was right. I knew it, there was still a part of me that wanted to go at this alone so if anyone got hurt it would be me.

"Hooker, we are in this. He hurt my best friend and killed our sister. I have power now. I will NOT sit here and do nothing."

God, I love Troy.

"I caused all of this." Monique's voice held so much shame it very nearly broke my heart. I saw a tear roll down her cheek.

"So many good witches died because I was careless. I refuse to let him get away with it."

"Love, I'm beyond angry with you about even thinking of ditching us. But we are going to do this. We are going to finish this together."

Talk about a ragtag group.

I started laughing. I honestly couldn't help it. They all just stood, staring at me, gaping.

"Sorry," I could barely speak between whoops of laughter. I was on the edge of hysteria. "We are a bad joke. A drag queen, werewolf, witch and Druid all walk into a bar …" I was overcome by snorts and fits.

"Lord help her, she's lost her mind," Troy commented, trying to stifle a smile.

After the moment passed, I tried to center myself. Here we were, the four of us in an open field. This moment could be the last the four of us would even be alive.

"Tomorrow is the day. You will call him and we will do our part. This will be over soon," he murmured as he kissed the spot just under my ear. The feel of his warm lips on my soft skin caused a shiver to run the length of my body. He growled in response.

"Oh no! She trembles, you growl, I know what comes next. And nuh-uh. Not happening. Keep ya drawers on!" Troy chided.

I rolled my eyes at Troy, and Reid laughed low in his chest, sending a pleasing vibration through me.

Okay, so I guess it was settled. Tomorrow we would be heading north. Tomorrow was D-Day. Delaney Day. I hoped Reid's plan worked. I mean it was iffy at best, especially since it hinged on Troy.

"Delaney, have you ever tried to shift with your clothes on?" Reid's question caught me off guard. I just blinked at him.

"Uh, no. I guess I just assumed that I couldn't."

"Delaney, our ability to shift is linked to the beast. Yours though, I think it's magical."

Shit, if I could, it would be a huge game changer. I saw it in his eyes. He was thinking the same thing I was. How huge this would be.

"Well?" Both Troy and Monique called at the same time.

I took a few steps back. The loss of Reid's physical touch and warmth was always something that had a profound effect on me. Those feelings alone spoke volumes about how much I loved him.

When I shifted, it never felt like shifting to me. It was more falling into this new form. My beast was there, but it was as though she were an afterthought now. I took a deep breath, closed my eyes, and fell into my form. I opened my eyes and squinted at the bright orange of the late-afternoon setting sun. It took my eyes some time to adjust.

In what had to have been the first time since I was turned, I didn't feel like my beast was thrashing against its cage trying to beat its way out. I felt like I had total control. I felt like I could finally take an unrestricted breath.

I looked down and expected to be covered in clothes or at the very least have them pooled around me. But, there was nothing. I looked up to Reid.

"I had a feeling." He smiled and crossed his arms over his chest.

"What, that she could change with her clothes on?" Troy asked.

He nodded and said, "That, but mainly that Delaney doesn't play by any of the rules."

I fell back into my human self. I swayed a little on my feet. Two quick changes left me a little breathless and dizzy. I felt a strong hand on my shoulder ground me. Shifting with my clothes on, as silly as it may seem, really could be the biggest key in killing Mitch. It very well might be my ace up my sleeve.

We spent the rest of the daylight helping Troy and making sure he had a good grasp on what we needed him to do. He really was picking this up remarkably quickly. I told him how impressed I was. He brushed the praise off, like I knew he would, but there was a hint of a glow from him.

He had fireballs pretty well handled. A drag queen who could shoot fireballs. I could only cackle at the absurdity of the situation. He was even deflecting attacks from both Monique and me. Troy's brow was covered with a sheen of sweat and he looked to be flagging.

He held up a hand and waved it in submission.

"That's it, bitches. I'm done!"

"You did really well, Troy," Monique commented.

"And you didn't need me to threaten someone this time!" I quipped. I gave him my best saccharin-sweet smile. To which he flipped me the bird. Then his smile faded and a puzzled look fell over his face.

"So, I have a question." Lord only knew what was about to come out of his mouth.

"Should we brace ourselves?" I asked before he could continue.

"Haha, funny. But really." He looked at Monique and continued, "If the inner circle of the Coven is looking for Delaney and they had a good idea where she was, based on Reid, then why aren't they here yet? I mean, don't get me wrong, I'm glad they aren't the cherry on top of this shit storm. But, why aren't they here?"

I blinked because I hadn't even thought to question that. Both Reid and I looked to Monique. Reid had a look of shock on his face. Clearly, he hadn't thought to ask this question either.

Monique shifted on her feet slightly as though the question rubbed her the wrong way.

After a moment, she spoke, "They did send someone for you. Me." It was like a punch to the gut.

Reid went rigid next to me and he stepped in front of me. I put a hand on his back. He seemed to soften slightly at my touch.

"Explain." Reid's tone beseeched no argument. I sidestepped him so I could see Monique. She seemed so crestfallen.

"I understand this isn't one-hundred percent what I told you, but please give me the benefit of the doubt."

"We're listening," Troy responded in a clipped tone.

She took in a deep breath and explained, "They sent me to find you before you even called me. I made up my mind after Reid came to the Coven, and we found out it was Mitch, that I would leave the inner circle. Before I could though, I found out about the breeding program. I was sickened when they told me that was their main driving force for wanting you. Then they tasked me to find you. And I thought that I could keep them away from you if they thought I just hadn't found you yet. I know I should have told all of you, but I did not want you to doubt my motivations. I'm here to kill Mitch and stop the Coven. Then you called me."

Our eyes met; hers were utterly unreadable.

"I knew it was bad, Delaney, I just wanted you to trust me to help you. I swear to you, I'm here to help." There was something off in her tone. I couldn't place it. Maybe it was my doubt or even the result of Mitch warping how I saw people. I nodded at her, not able to say anything.

Reid cleared his throat and said, "I believe you. I just wish you would have told us before now. But it does makes good sense to keep them off our backs until Mitch is dealt with."

When he growled the words *"dealt with."* It really left no question just how he wanted to deal with him.

"Welp, Little John …" Troy said, slapping Reid on the back, "Let's go kill the sheriff of Nottingham."

"Does that make you Robin Hood?" Reid asked, trying not to smile.

"Uh … duh? Have you seen my legs in tights? It's pretty epic."

We all tried to make this a serious situation, but with the image of Troy in tights, we all burst out laughing.

The ride home was filled with silence. I knew when I got to Troy's we would finalize details and I would make my call. I had to trust that it would all come together. Because it had to. I wanted my face to be the very last thing that Mitch saw before he drew his last breath. And I wanted it to be filled with a smile.

MiTCH SALDANA

EiGHTEEN

THE SCENT OF blood and piss greeted me. *God, how I love the scents of fear and carnage.* The stagnant air of the basement held on to scents as though it were Velcro. And with the two we had down there, the air was so thick with it I could almost feel it coat my tongue. I licked my lips as I descended the stairs. My beast seemed to stir with each step. It was all I could do not to lap the air with hopes of a small taste. The dark stairwell ended at a padlocked door. The door was laced with silver, as were all of the doors in this place. I slipped the small silver key into the lock and jerked it open. Had that been a normal lock, I would have smashed it to bits, but silver seemed to suck all of

179

the strength and energy out of any werewolf; I was no exception.

The door opened to a short corridor with four rooms off of it; two on either side of the hallway. There was a larger room at the end of the corridor and that was where I was going. That was where the delicious scents were emanating from. I could hear the faint sounds of screaming, the sound of a blunt object hitting flesh, and the wet sound of the impact. It was like Christmas. I have had these two for a few days and each time I could inflict my frustration and pain on them was like a gift.

The door was unlocked, as I knew it would be. When I wasn't here, my second and third were. My new third was especially enthusiastic about his brutality. I couldn't be prouder of him.

The room was brightly lit. When doing this type of thing, one needed to see every last bit of the evidence left upon the body. Mark was chained with a mix of iron and silver. He was splayed out on the left-hand side of the expansive room. His arm, which had been lovingly severed, had begun to grow back. It would be fun to sever it again and again, along with other body parts. His wife hadn't fared as well. Humans were just so fragile. We had disposed of her in short order. Her begging and pleading was annoying and got on my nerves. Now, there was one. And his torture could go on for eternity. The thought made me smile.

"Alpha, you look rested," Dillon remarked.

I surveyed the room and its occupants more fully now that my eyes had adjusted to the bright lights. I was wrong. My second wasn't here. My third and Anderson were here.

"I am, thank you. How is our guest?" I asked, walking over to Mark, who was slumped against the wall.

"Passed out, and it's no fun when he's unconscious," Dillon answered, heading over to a large metal table in the middle of the room.

There were several instruments laying on it and most of them were covered with a thick coat of blood. I wanted to run my tongue along the slick metal, lapping it clean of the delicious gleaming liquid. I resisted, but only just. Dillon flicked a hand under the faucet and water flowed forth, washing the sticky red substance clean from his finger. *What a waste*.

"Anderson, you talked to Delaney, correct?"

"Yes, sir, I did. She thinks the weres are rioting against you, and we will allow her to railroad you," he replied in a straightforward tone.

"And you told her we would be coming down there."

"Yes, sir, I did."

"And she bought it?" I questioned with a raised eyebrow.

"Oh yeah. Without a question."

"Good. Dillon, how many from the pack do we have going down there?"

He shifted uncomfortably on his feet. He didn't even try to hide the discomfort he felt with this question. I knew no matter what his answer would be, I wouldn't like it.

"I have contacted everyone a number of times. Out of the thirty or so we have left, I have heard from twenty."

"Well, that's better than I thought you were going to say."

"Um … well … of those twenty, only eight confirmed. So, that makes about twelve."

Ah, there it was. The news that would piss me off. With Delaney, I had the means to take down the Coven, organize the weres and obtain power. Yet, there was my pack, jumping ship thinking there would be no reprisal. This pack was once the largest in the States. Now? We were nothing but a joke. I was seething. I could feel the anger building. Then I had an idea. I smiled with how simple it was. All of the pack knew how Mark betrayed me. They knew I had him, but they had no idea just what was being done to him. I would just have to show them.

"Anderson, go get a camera. Dillon, I think it's time they all see what will happen if they choose not to come."

I would send each and every member a reminder of just why it was not a good idea to say no to me, why you don't fuck with me. I clenched and unclenched my fists. Without a word, Anderson left the room.

"We have very little time before the full moon. We need to have as much power as possible. The wolf I have observing Delaney said that she had two incredibly powerful witches with her. Both who look to have power equal to that of the inner circle. They could prove to be an issue. Also, he said Delaney has gotten stronger now that she has been mated to Reid." I snarled the last words. I should have forced her when I had the chance.

Did I honestly think the four of them could take twelve of us? It was possible, but not likely. Delaney's power was out of this world. She couldn't kill me. I was her maker. It was physically impossible for her to do so. The other three could though, and would likely try. Monique, the dumb twit, had settled her loyalty with them, and she had left the inner circle to do so. She was so undyingly loyal to the group of old assholes that it somewhat surprised me. But there was nothing like a scorned ex-lover.

"Yes, sir, I think this video is a good idea but, um …" He trailed off, seeming to take care with his words. Good too, as I was in a volatile mood and would likely chain him up with Mark. "… Um, to be honest, I think it might be too late. The pack is restless. Some of them didn't like the witch being here and didn't agree with it. The ones who did, well, now that she's gone, they don't trust that you can deliver on the promises you have made."

My fist hit the metal table. The whole table buckled and caved in at the impact.

"Promises! I'm their fucking alpha! When I say jump, they fucking ask if they can get me a coffee first!" I was roaring and didn't care.

"I know, alpha. I'm in this with you. I'm just telling you that since the night you changed the witch, we lost half our numbers. And because you were engaged with her, you did nothing about the loss. They are losing respect and fear of you."

My vision went red, and before I could stop myself, I had Dillon pinned against the wall with my hand around his throat. I could squeeze him here so fast that his neck would crunch and squish between my fingers. With a jerk of my hand, his head would pop off like a grape. My beast threw itself at the bars of the cage. He was desperate to get out and kill. I was only moments away from letting him.

"Mitch ..." The word was strangled.

It was an annoying buzz in my ear.

"Mitch." The word penetrated the red haze.

I released my grip slightly. I could feel a frantic pulse just under my fingertips. I breathed in a deep lung full of air. I released the grip fully and backed away. It wasn't Dillon, it was his words. They were the truth. He leaned forward, gasping for air. There was a slow, methodical laugh that filled the room. It was Mark. He had clearly awakened and found something funny about the situation. Now I had something I could take all of this pent-up aggression out on.

I smiled at him. "Oh, it's a shame your wife is no longer with us. You know how much I love a human's blood." He yanked his chains, trying to lunge for me. In his weakened state and with the silver that was both confining him and coursing through his veins, he wasn't able to do more than annoy the hell out of me. He was like a fly buzzing just by my ear, and no matter how many times I swatted at it, it never went away.

"Mitch, you're an evil bastard."

"Mark, I'll take that as a compliment."

"You know I would be shocked if you had even a third of the pack backing you. It's pathetic really."

I knew what he was doing. He was goading me, trying to get me to lose my cool and kill him. Oh, he would die, just not anytime soon. Maybe I would overnight his head just like I did his hand. The thought of the look of horror and fear on Delaney's face got me hard as fucking steel. I wanted her to fear me. I could honestly say I got off on it.

I was about to respond when Anderson came into the room with a small flip camera. I smiled at him, then back at Mark.

"Are you ready for your close-up?" I asked, giving him my best predatory smile. I licked my lips at the thought. I couldn't help it.

"Bring it, asshole."

Oh, bring it, I will. Anderson hit the record button, and I unbuttoned my shirt. No need to get ugly stains all over the white button-down. I breathed in a deep breath and, to Mark's credit, there wasn't a hint of fear. But there would be, oh there would be. And I couldn't wait.

I NEARLY BROKE the door with how fucking pissed off I was. That asshole hadn't even had the decency to piss himself or scream the whole time I tortured him. But with little time, the video would have to do. It would rally nearly twenty wolves, because it had to. We had no other options. I threw my blood-covered clothes in the laundry and grabbed some athletic shorts and a shirt. I was rounding the corner and nearly ran smack into Anderson.

"What the hell are you doing up here? You should be down …"

He had a phone in his hand and looked out of breath.

"Sir, um, it's the phone. I mean, it's for you. It's her." His eyes were darting to gauge my reaction.

My own eyes went wide in shock. Why the hell was she calling me? I grabbed the phone. *Do not crush it, Mitch. Reign it in.*

"Hello, Delaney." I closed my eyes, remembering the last time I said those words to her. I'd been looking at her glowing silver eyes. The only wolf I knew whose eyes glowed silver, not green. It was so erotic.

"Mitch." Her tone was flat and emotionless. Not at all surprising, but I liked hearing the fight in her voice.

"And to what do I owe the pleasure?" There was no way this was a call to check up on me.

"Mitch, listen, I don't have any time. I want you to swear to me you won't hurt any of them."

"Go on." My brows furrowed. Just where was she going with this?

"I have a plan to get away and come up there tonight. But, the only way I'll do it is if you meet me where and when I tell you, and you vow not to hurt them."

"Why not just come here?"

"Because I don't trust that you won't hurt me. Look, I'll be alone. I know you have a wolf here keeping tabs on me. He will tell you that I'm leaving alone. You meet me where and when I say and then swear to me neither you nor your pack will go after Reid or my friends. Then I'll go willingly, without a fight."

This was a trap. I was not dumb enough to think there wouldn't be something waiting for me. But, why now? Why not wait until they were all at their full power? None of this made sense. I could have a plan of my own though. If I had time to get the video out to the pack, I could maybe have some members there.

"Here's the deal. If you don't meet me, I'll go seek aid from the Coven."

"Why?" I asked. I just didn't trust this.

"Because I love my friends and care if they die. I know how many wolves you have, and we can't possibly handle them." She sighed. "Look, I just want them safe. I can get away tonight and meet you. I want to be one-hundred percent sure that you won't go after them. So, I want you to meet me at a neutral location. This is your last chance before I go to the inner circle." She sounded as if she believed what she was saying.

She had no idea that I only had the support of about a third of the pack. I could just not show up and then she would go to the fucking Coven. Two or three witches I could take, but the whole inner circle? Not a chance.

"I'll send someone for you." I could send Anderson.

"No. Are you a coward?"

"Fine, I'll meet you. But know, if this is some misguided attempt at a trap, it won't work," I warned.

The address she gave me was an hour outside of Atlanta. In the sticks.

"I'll refrain from killing them as long as this is on the up and up, Delaney. But if it isn't, I swear I'll do worse than kill them." My tone was calm and even.

I waited for a response, I only heard the faint buzz of an open line. I hung the phone up and looked up to meet Anderson's eyes. He raised an eyebrow in question.

"We don't believe her, do we?" he asked.

"Fuck no. Listen to me very carefully. I want you to get that video out to all of the pack. And tell them if they aren't there, what happened to Mark would be a holiday compared to what will happen to them." He turned to go do as I asked.

"Anderson." He turned, waiting for my instruction. "If they don't come, you will be the one on the chopping block. I'll assume your note didn't inspire."

"Yes, sir," he replied.

I inhaled and caught the scent of his fear. He disappeared down the hallway, but that spike lingered. I let my eyes slide shut and enjoyed the sharp scent. Tonight would be the night this ended. I had no doubt that it would end in my favor. Delaney had no idea the rules of the game she was playing. In the end, I would do as I have always done. I would win, because I made the rules of this game.

I opened my eyes, knowing they were glowing green with anticipation. I had a game to get ready for. I smiled at the thought of tasting her again. Checkmate, Delaney

NiNETEEN

"TYLER, GOOD TO see you again," I said, shaking the were's hand. He was a fairly tall man with dark-brown hair and matching eyes. I met him when I was dealing with Mitch. I didn't recognize him at our last encounter though and nearly ripped his throat out. This was the wolf who had been spying on us for the last few days. Little did Mitch know, Tyler, his resident tech guru, was displeased with how he was treating the pack. He was our in, and he was how we would break Mitch's pack up within hours. He was out of town when Mitch started on his killing spree and then bided his time to find a way to get out from under the alpha.

"Same here, Reid." His eyes darted from me to the three others. They lingered on Delaney for a moment before returning to me. He held a look of sympathy.

"Troy, Monique, this is Tyler. He is one of Mitch's wolves. He was sent to spy on us." Monique's eyes went wide and Troy's lips dipped into a frown.

"It's a good thing too. Or else I wouldn't be able to help you," He replied, eyeing each of us in turn.

"Help us? Why?" Troy asked.

He explained what he told Delaney and me the day we went out to run. I thought back to the moment I nearly slammed her against that tree and almost ate her alive. I shook my head to try to get the thoughts out of my mind. That was the last thing I needed to think about right now.

Once Tyler finished his explanation, his gaze went to the side of the wall just beyond me. He tilted his head up, exposing his throat; he was submitting to me. I stifled a growl. The gesture was noted and I clamped my beast down. It wanted to grasp the flesh between its jaws and reprimand the disobedient wolf, but I choked the urge back.

"Tyler, what can you offer us? How can you help?" *Why should we trust you?* I didn't add, but implied.

"I know half of the pack isn't behind Mitch. He had Anderson, his little bitch, call you and give you some conspiracy theory. The truth is, very few people agree with what Mitch did, and the vast majority of them are ready to turn on him. Reid, I told you all of this. Nothing has changed. I no longer recognize him as my alpha." I could hear the truth in his words.

"Have you been able to contact the pack?" Delaney had spoken the words before I had the chance.

"I have called many of them. The rest I'll send an email to. They will show up," he explained. He seemed to believe in his ability, but I, however, was not convinced. I looked over to Delaney, She didn't look convinced either. *Smart girl.*

"Why should we trust you? This whole story seems to be a little easy," Delaney asked.

We all seemed to ask this question in one form or another. I couldn't speak for everyone, but I was waiting for the other shoe to drop.

"Look, I came to you. I'm sure you knew I was here watching you. Reid, I was not in a position to go against him until now. And, you know it's not like leaving was an option." He was trying not to get defensive, but it came through in his tone.

"What's to say these people you contact won't go running, tail tucked, to Mitch?" Troy asked.

"Nothing. But he is the maker of all of us, so the likelihood of that is low, as half of the pack would love the chance to kill him."

"Delaney called and set up a meeting with him, assuring him that we wouldn't be there. I'm going to have to trust you to take my mate up there. We won't be far behind, but still. Do you see why I'm questioning your motives?"

"Reid, I understand. If there were a way for me to have you trust me, I would do it."

There was a faint buzzing noise. Tyler's eyes went wide. He fumbled in his pocket and retrieved his phone. He held up a hand gesturing for us to be silent. He swiped the phone and pressed it to his ear.

"Yes, sir."

His tone was a little too low for me to hear, but it was Mitch. Tyler must have had the volume on low.

"Yes, sir, I can do that."

Pause.

"You can send out a mass email if you like, sir. The contact list is there. It has every member's email."

Pause.

"Okay, sir."

He hung up the phone and slipped it back into his pocket.

"That was Mitch. He has some video he wants the pack to see. I thought he wanted me to send it, but he is going to send it to the pack via our newsletter."

"What is the video?" I asked, already knowing the answer.

"I don't know, he didn't say. He just said it was meant to rally the troops."

"Can you intercept the letter before it goes out?"

Tyler was a genius when it came to technology. He was one of the youngest of Mitch's wolves and he was turned because of his abilities.

"I need to go get my laptop from my truck. I'll be right back." He ran out of the room as though his pants were on fire. We all just looked at each other, trying to gauge our feelings about the situation.

"I don't see another choice. If Mitch has some scare tactic to get the pack involved with what happens tonight, we have to trust this guy." It was hard to disagree with Delaney's point.

"I …" I started, but was cut off as Tyler came barreling back in the room with a large shoulder satchel? Bag? Who the hell knew what those things were called.

He opened his bag and pulled out a large industrial-looking laptop. He plugged it in and powered it up. After a few moments, he began fiddling with the keys. His expression was completely focused.

"What is the Wi-Fi password?" he asked, not looking up from his screen.

"Oh, okay, it's: capital B-i-t-c-h-p-e-a-s," Troy said confidently.

"Your Wi-Fi password is, Bitch peas?" I asked Troy. What the fuck did that even mean?

He raised his brow and squared his shoulders as he replied, "Yes, it is, because, bitch peas." The last two words made it sound like he was saying bitch please. *Ah, okay, now I get it.* I just shook my head at him.

"Oh my God, Troy, I can't even handle you right now," Delaney muttered, trying not to smile. "You have no goddamn sense." He just shrugged. I returned my attention to Tyler. He was smiling, but still typing away. After a few minutes, Tyler's gaze tore from the screen and went to mine.

"Okay. There is a feature that I put on the newsletter that makes it so I'll have to approve anything that isn't sent from this computer. When I get that notification, I'll intercept and encrypt the old video, then send out the new one to everyone."

"Wait, make sure you send the legit thing to Mitch and his lapdogs," Delaney added.

He nodded as his fingers began an intense and somewhat methodical dance with the keyboard. His gaze was locked and completely focused. He was in his zone. I knew that kind of focus, when I was tracking someone on a case.

"Okay, everything is in place. When he uploads the video, there will be a prompt telling him that he needs the approval of the creator, me, to send it out."

"That should piss him off," I said smiling.

"What if …" Delaney started, but was cut off as soon as Tyler's phone began buzzing. I held up my hand to make sure everyone shut the hell up. Delaney scowled at me. She had such a cute scowl. I didn't want to die a swift and painful death, so I refrained from telling her that.

"Hey, boss," Tyler said, as he put the phone to his ear.

Pause, I could hear Mitch's voice rumble past the speakers. The tone was too low to make out clearly, despite my best effort.

"Yeah, boss, sorry, it's a feature with the newsletter. I'll approve it. You'll see it in your email in a few. Also, Delaney has been packing and just sent everyone off. She's alone. How would you like me to proceed?"

Pause and yet more rumbles from the phone.

"Got it." He hung up the phone.

"Am I the only one who says goodbye on the damn phone anymore? It's so obnoxious," Delaney chided.

I could only smile. Maybe it was a wolf thing or a guy thing.

"Don't laugh at me." Her eyes were narrowed at me.

I shrugged and pulled her close. I placed a small kiss on her lips and she softened against me. The feel of her little body melting into mine would be something I would never take for granted again. Her heart fluttering against my palm was a feeling I lived for.

"Don't look at her like that!" It was Troy's voice who seemed to break the spell between Delaney and me.

I raised an eyebrow in question.

"Oh, when you look at her like that the next thing we know you'll be hauling her off to get boinked." He was indignant and it made me laugh.

"I don't …"

"Got it!" Tyler exclaimed. He was impressed with himself. I returned my attention to him. "Now, what is this video?"

Though I couldn't see the computer screen, I could hear it. It was Mitch.

"Obviously, you forget who your alpha is. I think it's time you remember just who it is you will be pissing off. There is a time and address along with this email. If you aren't there, I'll do what I'm about to do to each and every one of you in turn." His voice was tinny and a little distorted from the speakers, but it was him. We all held a breath. Tyler turned his laptop so we could all see the small screen. I squinted to make out just what I was seeing.

It was Mitch and someone else chained to a wall. Who the hell was that? Delaney's hand flew to her mouth as if to stifle a scream. I looked at Tyler, who also looked sick.

He must have seen the question in my eyes, because he answered me with one word.

"Mark."

And then it began. This went so far beyond a simple beating. This was the most brutal torture I'd ever seen. I'd seen some things in my long life, but this was beyond all of them. It was clear Mitch was enjoying it. It was hard to hide his slow, panting breaths and his erection pressing against his pants. Was this what it was like for Delaney? Had he been aroused when he beat her? I looked over at her. Tears were streaming down her face, but she refused to look away. No doubt she blamed herself for this. How? How could she possibly go through one more thing and still come out on the other side unscathed? I returned my attention to the screen. Mitch picked up a small knife and walked over to Mark.

"Nope. Hell, no. Naw," Troy said, standing up. He threw his arms in the air and sprinted to the bathroom. Garrett followed him. I soon heard the sound of the two men fighting. I could guess what it was about.

"Shut it off," I told Tyler. We didn't need to be reminded of his brutality. I didn't need everyone to see just what would happen if we failed. And as much as I didn't want to admit it, failure was a very real possibility. Tyler closed the computer. I just sat there and stared at the laptop. God, now was not the time to be questioning if we could do this.

"Delaney, I know you want to be the one to kill him, but I may have to fight you for the right." It was Monique who spoke first.

"Tyler, we need to record our own video and email. Only send it to those whom you know will want to stand against Mitch."

"They need to see the power we have. They need to know if they stand with us they will be on the right side." Delaney seemed not the least bit shaken. If anything she seemed more resolved. *That's my girl.*

"We can do it with my phone. But we need to make it fast. We need to leave for the meeting place. It will take about three hours."

"And we need to get there sooner. If what I have planned is going to work we need to set up," I added.

The video only took a few minutes to complete once Tyler uploaded and sent it. After a few more minutes, Tyler's phone began blowing up with text messages. I looked at Delaney, who had been quiet. I stood up and took her hand. I only had a few moments with her before everything would hit the proverbial fan. I led her up the stairs to our room. We didn't have the kind of time I would have liked, but I needed to show her how I felt. I needed her to feel me in every way I could. I needed more than anything for this moment to last; for it to be a memory. If something happened, there would be nothing left unsaid.

I pulled her to me and held her. She wasn't trembling. She was vibrating, nearly tingling with power.

"Are you okay?" I whispered.

"Nothing about this is okay. God, Mitch was aroused when he beat Mark. I thought it was just me. But it was the act. He's sick." Her arms tightened around me.

I tried to tamp down on my anger. I had no idea about the details of what Mitch had done to her other than the fact he didn't force her to sleep with him. Had she stayed much longer he would have, I had no doubt.

I grabbed her face and cradled it between my hands. I wanted her to see what I was about to say, I wanted her to feel the power of it.

"I love you. I have no idea what will happen tonight, but I know no matter what, I love the woman you are right now, and I'll love the woman you become." Now, I just had to show her. And show her well.

DELANEY HAGEN
TWENTY

I PULLED AWAY and narrowed my eyes at him. "This better not be a goodbye fuck."

His eyes widened at my use of the word fuck. *Where had that come from? I have lost any semblance of a filter.*

"No, love, we don't have that kind of time," he purred as he pulled me closer.

I softened into him. Heat surged to my sex and I grew damp for him. The man had a direct connection to my libido that bypassed my brain. He inhaled a deep breath. The feel of his nearness and the knowledge of what he was doing made me weak in the knees.

"I can smell you." Those four words propelled me back to our almost first time. The time Troy stopped us. I tried to stifle a moan, but it slipped out. I seriously couldn't help my emotions and reactions to this male. *Hell, I don't think I ever will.*

"Oh? Do you like what you smell?" My voice was quaking. I knew goading an aroused werewolf may not be a smart idea, but I only had one fuck to give, and it involved me and him on that bed. Or floor. Or standing pinned against a wall.

His hand flew to the back of my head and he took a fist full of hair and yanked my head back, exposing my throat. He ground himself against me and I could feel just how hard he was, and sweet mother of God, I was nearly dripping for him. I felt his tongue trace a slow, wet line from my jaw down my neck.

I whimpered. I needed more. *I would never get enough of him.* I felt his free hand trace down my front and stop at my right breast. He cupped it and found the nipple in short order. He rolled the distended flesh between his thumb and finger, causing me to cry out. His slow laps turned into soft sucking and then he bit, hard. Not breaking the skin, but enough to make me

207

praise the gods he was holding me up. I was quickly becoming a puddle of my former self.

"Delaney! You need to go!" Troy called out while banging on the door. "And as much as everyone in the greater Savannah area enjoys hearing you and Reid go at it, you have a date with destiny."

I wanted to yell at him. In fact, I was close to telling him to go fuck himself, but he was right. There was no way I'd tell him that though; if his head got any bigger he would have trouble getting out of the house.

I groaned. Reid rested his forehead against mine. We both stood there, not knowing what to say. Every time I went to say something like: I love you, I need to go, be careful, or please don't die; the words seemed to fall flat. What does one say to someone they love? I didn't want to leave him wondering or questioning. I opened my mouth to tell him some long diatribe of my feelings, but he stopped me with a kiss.

He turned and walked over to the nightstand and pulled something out. It looked like a small box.

He met my eyes and he gave me a shy smile. He handed me the small box. My heart was racing. *Calm it down, Delaney, sheesh it's just a box*. I slowly lifted the lid. Sitting inside was a small white gold necklace. There were two charms nestled in the center of the chain: a small silver lightning bolt and a gold paw print. The charms were so delicate. It was beautiful. The lightning bolt was cut in a way that when the light hit it, it seemed to spark. I looked at him. He was studying my reactions. I plucked the necklace up and handed it to him. He took it without question and I turned my back to him and lifted up my hair.

He secured the chain and I turned to face him. He fingered the charms as he spoke, "Lightning for you. And a wolf print for me. You and me, Delaney."

I threw my arms around him, knowing this could be the last time. I knew I would do anything for this moment to be the first of many more to come. First, we had a few things to deal with. Mitch being number one.

We reluctantly went down the stairs. Everything else was a whirlwind. Reid, Troy, and Monique left before me. Tyler and I would leave about forty-five minutes after. Leaving me with someone Reid didn't trust one-hundred percent nearly killed him. And the goodbye between Troy and Garrett had Monique and me bawling like two big blubbering babies. I tried to tamp down on my feelings of guilt I had from so many of my friends putting their lives on the line. I knew they were willing to, but I hated to ask it of them.

"You ready?" Tyler asked, bringing me out of my own head.

"Yeah. Hey, how many do we have on our side?"

"Other than the five of us? Seven others. But that's iffy."

"I have one more question. Why? I mean, why go against your alpha?" I needed to know. No one just up and flips sides without a reason.

"Delaney, you have no reason to trust me, but believe me when I tell you Mitch has this coming. He forced this change on me, knowing I could have died. I didn't ask for this. He saw me as a tool to use and I'm done with it. When I saw what he did to you, what I unknowingly helped him do, I was ashamed. But I knew of all people, you would know how I felt." And I did.

I looked up to the sky and closed my eyes. *Look, I know you may have a plan for me, but please protect my friends. If I'm your daughter, please help us.* As if in answer, I heard the low, distant rumble of thunder.

"THIS ISN'T GOING to work," I said as we pulled up to the clearing.

"You're right. How about we leave and go get some beef and broccoli?"

I did a double take at Tyler. "What?" Was he serious? I mean I could eat, but now was not the best time.

He saw my confusion and shook his head. "Come on, and try to be afraid of me, please."

We picked this location because it was in the middle of nowhere, and it was an open field. Part of Reid's plan was forming a magical barricade cutting Mitch off from the rest of the pack. I wasn't sure how it would all come together, as we had only managed it twice in a five-foot circle; this circle was a hell of a lot bigger. And by we, I mean Troy. This was his only job. This had to work. I had no idea where the three were, but I knew it was close by. We weren't naive enough to think that Mitch would believe I was here on my own. The point of doing it this way was to throw him off.

God, this is going to be a clusterfuck! Shut up, Delaney, you pessimist.

There were a few things we had on our side. I could shift with clothes on. I could kill him or at least I thought I could. And we had wolves or at least I hoped we did. I could see Troy's reaction to my thoughts. He'd throw his hands up and yell, "Well, that's it, we dead!" And I didn't think I could argue with him. I shook my head to try to get my self-doubt and the negative thoughts to dissipate. I didn't hear a car, but the hairs on the back of my neck stood up. Mitch was here. It was time.

My throat was dry, and I could already feel the sparks falling from my fingers. *Try to keep calm, Delaney.* I took in a deep breath and held it, willing my heart to beat slower. I needed my body to be on-point. I needed my reflexes to be sharp. I needed to be the most powerful I'd ever been. And I needed it all to happen right damn now.

I slowly let the breath out. Then, I saw him. Whatever air was left in my lungs exited with a whoosh. Seeing him felt like a physical blow. I tried to keep the memories at bay, but failed utterly. The feel of his cool hands caressing me, then pinching, then hitting. The scent of his anger when he beat me and the sharp tang of his arousal as he inflicted as much pain as he could on me. If not me, then it would be someone else. The buck had to stop with me.

With great power, comes great responsibility. Okay, yes, a Spiderman quote popped into my head at that moment. Damn it, Uncle Ben was right. I had the ability, therefore I had the responsibility. It was my time. The fear was so real. I tried to keep myself from shaking, but it was fleeting. I was scared half to death. I knew the scent would work in my favor, but this was not a situation I was faking. This was real, soul-shaking the fear. I had to do this, I had to perform. I had to succeed.

Mitch was flanked by three men. Anderson, Matthew, and Dillon. Matthew was his next in command; of the four, other than Mitch, it was Dillon whom I knew was especially brutal. I could feel their excitement. Mitch, though, I could also feel his extreme lust and it nearly made me gag.

"Calm," Tyler whispered.

It was so low I almost missed it, but I knew it was that way because it was meant for my ears only. I nodded with just a small jerk of my head; he caught the motion. A strong gust of air sent my hair flying over my face. I tucked the strands behind my ears. Then I caught the scent of other wolves. The scents were too mingled to tell just how many, but there were a few.

This clearing was about fifty yards in diameter. I just prayed to whatever benevolent being was watching that I could do this. I prayed Troy and Monique were ready for this, because time was up.

"Tyler, was she alone?" Mitch yelled across the shrinking expanse of space that separated us.

"Yes, they will be here soon. We need to make this short." Don't play poker with Tyler, because the guy could lie. Or at least I hoped he was lying to him and not us. That thought doused me in another cold bucket of fear.

Mitch shook his head. That was ... well, odd. I looked at Tyler, who looked at me. He looked as confused as I felt. I heard a loud bang and then Tyler dropped beside me. Like a sack of fucking potatoes. I felt something warm spray across my face. *What the hell just happened?* I blinked, trying to understand what was going on. The images in front of me were not registering.

"Tyler." I reached up to wipe my face free of the smattering of mud. Wait, mud wasn't warm, was it? I glanced at my hand. It was dark, but I knew it was blood. I couldn't hear him breathing. A shot, even with a silver bullet, couldn't kill him, but holy shit. I took a step back; it was instinctive, but it showed weakness. I wanted to kick myself for doing it.

Only fifty feet separated me from them. This was not the plan. Something had changed, but I didn't know what.

"Awe, did the little traitor get a boo boo?" Mitch called. The blood in my veins turned cold. One of the wolves told him. That had to be it. *Shit. Shit. Shit!*

Play dumb? Or go on the defensive? "What the hell is going on, Mitch?" Dumb it was.

"Delaney, is every word that comes out of your mouth a lie?" His words were laced with venom. "I can't scent them, but I know they are here." I took advice from Mark and bleached everyone's clothes and

215

they each had a spray bottle to help. I had no idea if the wolves that surrounded us were on our side or not.

A few yards back, I saw a number of his pack coming into the clearing. My heart was pounding as though it had a drum solo at a rock concert. Maybe it would land a music deal and make me a shit ton of money. I shook my head. Damn inappropriate humor. There were six. None were behind me. Well, none that I could scent. Less than we thought, but ten was a lot more than four.

"Is that all the loyalty you could scare up?" Apparently, I had a death wish. You know what, fuck him. I was so done with rolling over with fear of this dickweed. I squared my shoulders and narrowed my eyes.

"Did your lap dogs see that nice hard-on you had going on while you were beating Mark?" He jerked at my words and took a step forward. I didn't even react. Point to me.

"Delaney, what do you hope to accomplish by taunting me? I know they are hiding out there with some plan that will fail. Come to me and I'll spare them." I saw the lie in his posture before I heard it in his words.

"Mark, Tyler, probably Mark's wife. All because they didn't want to be under a sick and demented monster. You know the moment you disagree with him you or someone you care about will be next," I spoke my words as I looked at each of the wolves in turn.

Mitch started laughing. The sound made my skin crawl. It reminded me of that feeling of running into a spider web that covered my whole body.

"Delaney, I see what you're trying to do, but my love, they know all of these things. That's why they won't go against me. They are under my boot and will heel to me alone." His words seemed to agitate five of the six men. My attention was torn from the men to a loud gasp I heard from Tyler. He had to have been coming back to himself. Not fully healed, but coming back.

Mitch's fists clenched and his mouth turned into a hard white line. I couldn't see his eyes before, but now they were glowing green. I didn't need to look behind me to know it was Reid. This was not the plan. *What the hell is he doing?* I felt his warm hand grasp the back

217

of my neck. There was no mistaking the possession of the gesture.

"I hadn't known for sure if Tyler betrayed me, but now, I do."

"So, you had him shot just for the hell of it?" I was incredulous. What the actual crap?

He ran a hand through his hair. The movement looked so innocent that I nearly forgot what a monster he really was. Even at this distance, I was reminded of what it felt like to have that same hand run over my skin. I shivered at the memory. Reid felt it and glanced down at me. He winked, then returned his attention to the men. He winked? The hell was that about? I didn't really see this as a winking moment.

"Reid, are you enjoying my sloppy seconds? Her taste is so sweet, isn't it?" he taunted, while he licked his lips.

Reid's grip tightened around the back of my neck, but he didn't say anything. I hadn't told him about the worst of the abuse by Mitch. I didn't know if I ever could. He didn't break me though, not fully. The bone had been broken and now it was set and healing.

"Shoot them and get it over with." Mitch waved a hand in our direction. I only had a heartbeat. I pulled my power from my core in a rush. Lightning flooded my entire body. The world seemed to slow down. I could feel the sparks covering my whole body. My vision changed from its normal dark shadows to a kind of inverted black and white. Everything that had been dark was now blazing white. In the time it took me to call my lightning forward, Reid dropped to the ground. Good thing too, because he would have resembled a charcoal briquette right about now. I knew I could block a magical attack and even a physical one, but a bullet? I threw my hands out and pushed all of my power out into a wall. My lightning acted more like a net, but right now I needed it to be a wall. I felt the impact, small and distant. I heard a scream. Not just a scream though, a blood-curdling scream of pain. Shit, had the bullet slipped through? I thought I stopped it, damn it. I dropped the wall. The men behind Mitch and his lapdogs were on fire, completely engulfed in flames. It was magical fire so the whole stop, drop, and roll thing wouldn't work, not if Troy didn't want it to. They tried to run off, but something held them in place. Then, in a rush, heat that stole every bit of moisture from my eyes hit the edge of the clearing, erupting in blinding flames. My eyes squinted at the bright intrusion.

Troy was nowhere to be seen. Reid ripped his clothes off and began his change. I had a choice, I could stand guard or rush the other wolves. I glanced to them. Mitch was nearly finished with his change, but the other men were standing over him. I made a decision and stayed put. I did pull my power into my hand and threw several lightning balls in their direction. None hit. *Where the hell is Monique?*

Mitch charged me. Shit, Reid wasn't done. I had only a moment. I reached into my pocket and felt the cool metal of a coin. I threw it down near Reid and ran at Mitch. Pulling hard on my power, I tried to throw everything I had at him, but he was fast and dodged everything. This wasn't going to work. Not like this. I was acting and thinking like a witch.

I ran full force at him, narrowing my eyes and focusing on his throat. I shifted as he lunged at me. He went flying over me. I turned as fast as I could and rushed him. I connected with my teeth sinking into his left hind leg. I pulled my power so that every time I contacted him it sent jolts surging through him. He ripped his leg from my jaw with a surprising amount of strength. White-hot pain hit my right side. The force of whatever hit me sent me flying several yards away from Mitch. I heard, more than felt, the snap of a rib breaking. I tried to take in a deep gulp of air, but the sharp pain in my side prevented anything. The world was spinning. I blinked up, trying to stop the world from caving in. Finally, after a few more blinks, I remembered where I was and flipped from my side to my feet. I winced at the pain that was now radiating throughout my whole right side.

The scene in front of me was surreal. Monique stood at the side of the circle of blazing fire trying to catch wolves, keeping them away from engaging in the fight. Tyler was moving now, but much like the six wolf-jerky assholes, he was in no condition to do anything. I could see Troy's faint silhouette through the fading fire wall. And surrounding him were figures that I couldn't quite make out. I blinked and stepped toward them. Fear. Fear that struck me as intense as a lightning bolt struck me at the sight of nearly ten wolves surrounding Troy. *Oh, God, no!* I glanced around, trying to find Reid. I spotted him near where I last saw Mitch. He was trying to fight off four wolves at once.

This was the hardest decision I ever had to make. I shifted to my human form and ran to Troy.

"Delaney!" I heard Monique's voice a fraction before I felt the teeth sink into my calf. I screamed. This couldn't be happening. There were too damned many of them and they were all changing so damned fast. I pushed my power out through my whole body. I only distantly heard the yelping of pain. *Fuck me, that hurt.* I couldn't think about that right now, I had to get to Troy. My vision flickered from its normal color to black and white and back again.

I ran. With every step, agony radiated from my calf up my whole goddamn leg. I was so close. I jumped through the fire, praying I had enough lightning around me to protect me from the flames. I staggered at the sight. The ten, wait nine, I didn't know how many, but they weren't attacking him, they were protecting him. I was astonished. Nearly the whole pack was here, and a good deal of them were on our side.

"D! I can't hold this wall much longer. Go get your man!" Troy's tone was frantic, but his words hit me. *Shit, Reid.* I ran back through the now painfully thin wall of fire.

"Monique! We need to help Reid!" I called to the Earth Witch. She pulled her power at the barbequed men and I saw roots begin to pin them in place. *Why hadn't she done that in the first place?* I didn't have time to think about that right now. I ran full force at the five wolves. It was hard to tell where one started and one began. I pulled my lightning out, and hurled a ball at one wolf. My guess was that it was Anderson. It hit him square in the side. He was ejected from the fray. One down, three to go.

"I'm here, love," I said mentally to Reid. He had Mitch at his front and who I thought was Matthew at his side. Where was Dillon? I glanced around, but didn't see him.

"Monique, take out Mitch!" I yelled. Maybe, if we all focused on him at once we could be more effective.

"My pleasure."

I shifted back to my wolf self and closed the distance between Mitch and me. Once again, I pulled my power from my core. I'd never used so much power, yet it was there for the taking. I launched myself at him, and never made it. I was stupid. I thought for just that moment that we had this. I was so wrong. Dillon had been sitting, waiting. He grabbed me in midair. When we landed, my throat was in his mouth. I felt his teeth sink into my neck. Warm blood spilled down my front, soaking my fur. I couldn't scream. The pain, my God, it was electric. My heart rate was frantic and with each beat I felt the trickle of blood pulse more. Shit. I was losing blood, and fast. I tried to get out of this. I really did. I fought, but with each moment I fought, Dillon's jaws only tightened. This wouldn't kill me. I was losing consciousness. I could feel myself passing out. I kicked again and again, but it did no good. Fuck me.

I looked to Reid. He was fighting both of the wolves off, but only just. Monique was helping him. Reid could do this. He could kill Mitch for me. I wasn't giving up; I was just so tired. If I just closed my eyes for one second, I could …

TWENTY-ONE

THIS FIGHT WAS more like a to-do list. Snap jaws. Protect my flank. Dodge teeth. At some point, the three wolves turned to two and then two turned to one. I tried to survey what was being done around me, but the constant engagement with Mitch made that nearly impossible. I saw flashes of Delaney's power and then of white fur. I caught glimpses of Monique's hands glowing green. I heard the snarls, growls and yelps of wolves fighting.

Tyler's wolves came through in the end. There were about nine or so of them. I didn't get a good count. They showed up just before I joined Delaney in the clearing. We knew Mitch would never really believe that she would be here without us. What we banked on was the amount of support he would get on short notice. The moon was waxing, but it was not at its apex; we were on equal footing. It was a now or never situation. This was a Hail Mary and every last person here knew it.

Mitch lunged at me. He caught the meat just above my shoulder with a tooth. But he didn't have the angle needed for a full-force bite. I tried to spare a glance to find Delaney, but Mitch was there at every turn. I needed to get rid of him. He attacked and this time I ducked my head. My jaws clamped down on his forepaw. My teeth bounced off bone and his momentum sent me staggering back a few steps. He thrashed wildly and, despite my best effort, he broke the grip I had on him. I snarled at the taste of his blood in my mouth.

"Love?"

No response.

"Delaney!" I called again to her mentally. Again, no response. I spotted a gray wolf with Delaney's limp fur-covered form seemingly dangling from his clenched jaws. She wasn't moving. My heart stopped. The world stopped turning. *Shit*. Her throat was in Dillon's jaws. I had so many of my own aches and pains I couldn't differentiate between what was mine and what I was feeling through our bond. All I knew was I had to get to her; there was no other choice. I refused to fail her again.

I charged Mitch, but he met me for every move I made. Monique was pelting Matthew, who was fast as a greased pig. Monique tried to catch him within a set of roots, but her magic wasn't made for something so fast. I faked right, but Mitch knew the move and went left. Other than surface wounds, there was little contact made. It almost seemed like he was holding me off so Dillon could get Delaney. In fact, I was sure that's what he was doing. No, this would NOT fucking happen!

My whole being stopped at the sight of Dillon, who was now shaking Delaney. I failed her once before. I handed her right to Mitch on a silver fucking platter and hell fucking no would I ever let that happen again! I rushed Mitch again. I didn't pull back this time. I didn't dodge his teeth – I took them full force. I connected with the side of his face, bit down blindly, and ripped. He yelped in pain. I didn't let up, charging nearly through him. I had to get to Dillon. I managed to hit Mitch with such force that it sent me on a direct path to Dillon. I had to help her. I hit the gray wolf with all of the force of a train. The impact sent the wolf flying away from Delaney, but I didn't let up. I was on him as he landed.

As far as size went, Dillon was about the same as Mitch. Both of them were smaller than me, but they were as fast as rats and just as sly. He was dazed. I used it to my advantage. I had a distant thought, why wasn't Mitch on me? I shoved it down and focused on Dillon, clamping my jaws down on his throat and crushing it. I felt the warmth of his blood coat my tongue and wanted to shudder with the pleasure of the tangy metallic flavor. I didn't have time to revel in the magical taste of his life force. I clamped down even harder and with a quick shake of my head his throat had been well and truly removed from his body. No, it wouldn't kill him, but it would put him out for a long while. He wouldn't have to worry, death was not far from him.

I whirled to face Delaney. She was now in human form. It wasn't her form that caused me to pause. It was the fact that Mitch was in human form cradling her in his arms. *How the fuck was he able to change so goddamned fast?* Seeing Delaney's limp body in his arms made something inside me snap. My gaze shifted to Monique, who had finally caught Matthew. He was fighting the confines of her bonds, so her attention was solely on him.

The night was filled with smoke from Troy's fire, the scent of burnt wood and flesh, and the sounds of fighting wolves. But right here and right now, the scene was filled with my mate in the arms of a monster. I could charge him, but then I risked hurting Delaney. Mitch met my eyes, and I knew he saw my struggle.

"What's wrong, Reid?" He was out of breath and blood rushed down his face from his missing ear down to his bare chest. We were both at a standstill. I could do nothing for fear of hurting my mate. I snarled at him, and he smiled in return.

"It was a shock to see her change with clothes on. But, no matter." His words grew distant. I felt something, a draw on my very being. Like the strength was being leached out of my body. I flicked my eyes to Delaney. The limp arm that hung over Mitch's hands began dripping with sparks. I knew how it felt to be shocked by her, yet he didn't seem phased.

As though she were rising up from the dead, her head whipped up and she jammed her hand against his chest. She screamed as I felt her lightning leave her. I felt it as though it were leaving me. The searing pain of her lightning left me feeling as though I was set on fire then dipped in a vat of acid. If I'd had the ability to scream out I would have, with the pure agony of the force of her power that I knew was flowing through me.

A flash of astonishment flashed across Mitch's face before he collapsed to his knees. Delaney fell to the ground and I ran over to her. She scrambled over and threw her arms around my neck; the scents, tastes, and sounds … God, everything stopped. The world could have stopped existing because I had her. She was whole, here, and she was mine. She was the reason I took each breath and why my heart beat.

I began my change. Our mental connection had been fried with whatever power she pulled from me. My skin seemed to rip apart and stitch itself back together. I rushed the change. It was still nowhere near what I saw Mitch do. I had to figure out how he managed that, but that was for another time. I changed and Delaney never let me go. It took me roughly two minutes to have that woman in my arms.

She was crying. No, sobbing. I grabbed her face with my hands. She was not a pretty crier, but God, it didn't matter. Sobbing meant breathing and breathing meant alive and alive meant mine.

"Shh, honey, I have you." I rocked her.

She hiccupped, but calmed. The yips and barks of wolves fighting had stopped.

"My brave girl. You're so strong," I crooned to her.

She looked at me and that's when I saw it. There, in her eyes that glowed silver, was the spark of lightning. This woman, my mate, had done something no one thought possible. She defied all of the rules. She was truly the beginning of something new. I slowly realized the wolves were surrounding us. Some had shifted forms, yet others remained as wolves. I held her tighter. I tensed to take whatever it was they would dish out. Delaney pulled away from me. I met her gaze. I couldn't understand her expression, but I trusted her to do what she felt she had to. I let my arms fall away from her.

"Reid, I have to do this. I have to end this." Her eyes flashed bright white, like the strike of a lightning bolt. Her tone was resolute. I stood eyeing the now nearly twenty wolves. Not one of them made a move toward her. She hummed with power. It wafted off of her in heat waves. I couldn't help but scent the fear in the air. They were afraid of her. *Good. They should be.*

I walked beside her. I would be beside her as she finished this. I would always be beside her. And that thought eased all of the pain and hurt like a soothing balm.

DELANEY HAGEN

TWENTY-TWO

PAIN? THERE WAS none. I knew there should be though. I'd very nearly had my throat ripped out and probably a dozen other bites that should be hurting me. But there was nothing, only the man lying at my feet. I knew the whole of his pack circled me. Yet it didn't matter. Nothing did. I looked down at the man, no, monster, at my feet. I pulled all of my power when I laid my hand against his chest. I pulled every bit of everything I could find. When I sent my lightning through him, I pierced his heart and burned a hole right through him. The air even smelled of charred flesh.

I knelt down next to Mitch. Somehow, he blinked at me. He looked incredulous. Well, as incredulous as a man could look who had a coaster-sized hole burned through his chest. He looked as though he couldn't believe that I'd done it. I took a page from his book and smiled at him, all teeth. I smoothed the hair from his brow. I wanted to be sure he saw everything that was about to happen. He needed to see my face. He worked his jaw up and down. He was trying to speak, but no words came out. I realized just what he was mouthing.

"You can't kill me." I knew without words, that's what he was trying to say.

I again gave him his own predatory smile, then knelt down to his cheek and kissed the damp flesh there. He had no idea how wrong he was.

I leaned in close to his ear and whispered the last words he would ever hear.

"Oh, but Mitch, you should know by now I don't follow the rules."

I grabbed his neck with a blood-covered hand. His eyes went wide in shock. I pulled on all of the power I had left and sent it as hard as I could out of the hand covering his neck. The ground shook with the force of my power.

I breathed in the scent of burnt flesh. Morbid? Yes. Satisfying? Hell fucking yes.

His eyes that were so focused on mine went distant. His head lulled off to one side as the ground was not perfectly level. I'd never been so happy to see a head detached from a body. Well, not that I'd ever seen that before. I stood up and turned to face the half circle of wolves. I could feel the residual power sparking from my fingertips. And now I could feel the pain. I could feel everything. I gritted my teeth against the intensity of it.

"You see your alpha? He's dead." My voice was hoarse, but I pushed through it.

Reid walked over and wrapped an arm around me.

"Who wants to be next? Because I have had one hell of a day." Okay, there was no freaking way I could do anymore. I was a moment away from passing out. But they didn't know that. And no, it was not some inspiring prophetic speech. I was lucky it was words coming out of my mouth and not a garbled mess of incoherent thoughts.

The pack had nearly all shifted back to their human forms. A tall lanky man, whom I'd not met before, stepped forward. I pulled on my power, but what had been a raging river was nothing but a slow trickle of static. He dropped to a knee and tilted his neck up to me. Then another followed and another, and so on. They were submitting to me. I swayed. It was all a little too much. I no longer had the ability or strength to stand on my own. Clearly, the blood loss was getting to me. Reid held me tighter.

He must have sensed how I was flagging because he said in a low tone, "Go home. Delaney or I will be in contact with all of you."

God bless that man.

Troy picked that moment to limp into my view. He gave me a shy smile. "You know when I had fantasies of being surrounded by naked men this wasn't what I imagined."

I laughed. I couldn't help it. I winced, and my hand flew to my ribs. *Shit, that hurt.* I sucked in a breath, and that too hurt.

"Sorry to disappoint," I rasped. I scanned the area for Monique. She was off to the side of the mass of the pack. She had Anderson and Matthew tangled in roots. I looked to Reid, who followed my gaze.

"Troy, help Delaney, please. I have work to do." His voice was a rumble, his eyes were locked on the two wolves.

He closed the distance and grabbed my elbow.

Before he left, Reid leaned down and kissed the top of my head and whispered, "I'm so damn proud of you." His words made my heart flutter.

I felt the loss of his touch, but it was dampened by the fact that I still had everyone important to me.

"Stop," Troy chided.

"What?"

"You're grinning like a damn fool."

I hit him lightly in the chest. He flinched.

"Shit, are you okay?"

"Yeah, Tyler's wolves really came through. A few of the assholes got past my guard, but damn, D, you should have seen me! I was on fire."

I raised an eyebrow at him.

We both started laughing.

"Stop making me laugh. It hurts."

Instead of a pithy retort, he pulled me into his arms and held me. I felt the soft shudder of his sobs. Emotionally, he was probably as done as I was. Thinking I, and everyone one I loved, would die had that effect on a person.

"I love you so damn much. I was so scared. I would have killed you if you died." We stood there holding each other, crying like babies. We both tensed at the screams of the two men; neither of us said a word. Finally, when I took in a deep breath, it didn't hurt. I could breathe in every sense of the word. Mitch was well and truly gone. My friends were all safe. But, I couldn't shake the feeling that I was waiting for the other shoe to drop.

Reid walked over to us. He now had jeans on, but no shirt. His chest was drenched in blood. I didn't even blink twice before I threw myself into his arms. His hand cradled the back of my head, and the other wrapped around my waist.

"Let's go home, love," he whispered.

I nodded, fearing I would burst out in tears again.

"Wait, what about the, um, bodies?" I asked, eyeing Mitch's limp form. I shuddered. I couldn't help it.

Reid opened his mouth to speak, but was cut off by a new voice.

"Don't worry about them. I'll take care of it." He was a handsome man, tanned with dark hair and green glowing eyes. He looked to only be a few inches taller than me. I shifted in Reid's arms to look at him more fully.

"And you are?" I questioned.

"I'm Dante. Tyler's partner. Oh and here, you threw this down near him just before you attacked Mitch. It protected him." His eyes were grateful, and I couldn't help but feel bad.

It wasn't a thought, just a happy accident. I took the coin that was now blank and shoved it in my pocket.

"It protected me as well, love," Reid added as he placed a kiss on the top of my head.

"Wait, what happened to the barbecued wolves?" I wondered aloud.

"Ah yeah well, they were easy to kill once they resembled beef jerky," Troy said, looking a little dazed. "Can we go home now? Because this queen is so done."

"Wait!" They all turned and looked at me. "Dante, find Mark. I don't know if he's even alive but find him." My body may have been trembling but my voice didn't waver a bit. He nodded and turned to walk away.

Reid ushered to the cars. Four people came into this fight, and four were going home. Life was good. At least for the moment. We still had the Coven to deal with, but right now, Mitch was dead, and that was good enough for me.

TWENTY-THREE

Two weeks later

Four minutes. That's how long the stupid thing took. My heart was racing and shit, was I sweating? Ugh, I was. I paced the small bathroom. Stupid!

Delaney, you can kill a big bad alpha werewolf, but this test has you freaking out.

Okay, I needed separation. I walked out of the bathroom and exited the bedroom. After everything had gone down with Mitch and his pack, the four of us went back to Troy's and, well, Reid, Monique, and I didn't leave. Troy said all the time how he needed his space, and we were up his ass, but he forgot I knew him. He loved having us there.

The pack had definitely been a harder subject. While the pack recognized that I killed the alpha, and they did submit to me, it wouldn't work. I wasn't a werewolf. I couldn't lead them. Reid, however, could. Especially after how they found Mark. Mitch hadn't killed him. He had left him alive, but broken. Mitch had done unspeakable things to him, leaving behind a shell of a man. Reid grumbled about being a lone wolf, but I think, deep down, he needed a pack and felt he owed it to Mark. Monique was biding her time with us as we tried to devise a plan of attack on the Coven. This task was proving to be super easy. Okay, no, that was a lie; it was hard as fuck.

"Reid!" I called out. No answer. I was shaking with nervous energy.

I walked down the stairs and looked around for him. Nothing. Where was he?

"He and Troy went out. They said something about eggplant parmigiana." It was Monique.

I frowned. My gaze slipped from her to the ceiling. My heart began to beat faster.

Calm down, Delaney!

"You okay?" she asked. Her tone was concerned, and she shifted nervously from one foot to the next.

I couldn't wait any longer.

"Yeah. Just need to go check something." I gave her a small smile and walked up the stairs. Each stair was a mountain. And dammit I was free climbing. One misstep and I felt like I would fall to my death. I walked into the bedroom and stopped just outside the bathroom door. My heart beat wildly, and I could hear the whoosh of blood rushing behind my ears. It was just a test. A little test. Would I be happy no matter what it said? I took a deep breath and reached for the knob when I felt a jabbing pain in my neck. Ouch, shit, what was that? I reached for the aching spot and felt wetness. I brought my hand up to examine the liquid and blinked at my hand, not understanding. Was it blood? Had I been hurt? I swayed, and the world started spinning.

I began a slow descent to the floor. Cool hands helped guide me down. Maybe I was just tired. That was it, I needed a nap. *Wait! No!* This wasn't right. I blinked, trying to clear my vision of fog.

Monique moved toward the bathroom door and stepped inside. She picked up the small test. Her mouth went into a hard white line. She tossed it in the toilet and flushed. *What did it say? Wait, what did what say?* The world began to pulse with each beat of my heart. She walked over to me and knelt. I didn't understand, what had happened?

"What …" I tried to speak, but the word came out garbled and drugged.

"Did you really think I could betray my family?" Her words bounced around my fog-filled skull. I could do nothing but blink.

My world shrank. I was just tired. I just needed to nap. That was it, a nap. Then I would understand. I closed my eyes and distantly heard Monique's voice.

"Goodnight, Delaney." Then everything melted away into deep blackness …

TO BE CONTiNUED iN THE
FiNAL BOOK OF THE
LiGHNiNG WiTCH TRiLOGY

THE
LiGHTNiNG PROGENY

Playlist for
THE LIGHTNING LEGACY

Ryn Weaver-
Promises
OctaHate
Stay Low
Sail On

Ed Sheeran-
One
Don't
Photograph
Tenerife Sea
Thinking Out Loud
I See Fire

Hozier-
From Eden
Work Song
Foreigner's God
In The Woods Somewhere

Matt McAndrew-
Wasted Love

Josh Turner-
Long Black Train

Kiesza-
Sound of a Woman (Delaney's song)

Evanescence-
Evanescence - (the whole self-titled album)

ABOUT THE AUTHOR

Emily Cyr is a stay-at-home mom turned writer. She holds a degree in middle grades education with certification in English and social science. She has always had a love of all things paranormal and fantasy, but it wasn't until Emily's husband said the words, "Why not?" that she considered putting her thoughts and ideas into the book, The Lightning Prophecy. This trilogy was just the start for Emily. It seemed to open a creative door that had been locked.

Emily has always been an avid reader. Through reading came her love of writing. The more she read, the more she knew she wanted to create her own world. Many of her first works were fan fiction.

Emily and her family currently reside in Jacksonville, Florida. She has an incredibly supportive husband. They have two sons, ages 4 and 3. Somehow, even with the demands of being a parent to two little boys, she finds time to escape to her fantasies and write them down.

Currently, Emily has two urban fantasy series out, but stay tuned via her web-site, www.EmilyCyr.com, for more!

44537380R00213

Made in the USA
Charleston, SC
30 July 2015